MW01167459

ROUGH & Tumble

THE UNIVERSITY OF ATLANTA SERIES

ROUGH & Tumble

THE UNIVERSITY OF ATLANTA SERIES

SHAE CONNOR

This book is a work of fiction. Names, characters, places, and incidents are the product of the author's imagination or are used fictitiously. Any resemblance to actual events, locales, or persons, living or dead, is coincidental.

Copyright © 2020 by Shae Connor. All rights reserved, including the right to reproduce, distribute, or transmit in any form or by any means. For information regarding subsidiary rights, please contact the Publisher.

Entangled Publishing, LLC
10940 S Parker Rd
Suite 327
Parker, CO 80134
rights@entangledpublishing.com

Embrace is an imprint of Entangled Publishing, LLC.

Edited by Amy Acosta
Cover design by Bree Archer
Cover photography by Morsa Images/Getty Images
KIKE ARNAIZ/Stocksy
caluian.daniel/Deposit Photos

Manufactured in the United States of America

First Edition November 2020

embrace

For Jamie, who asked me to write a story about "a ginger gymnast," lo, these many moons ago.

Chapter One

Hi, my name's Grant Clark, and I have managed to screw up my entire life. In triplicate.

Number one: I fell in love with my best friend.

Number two: I thought he was straight.

Number three: Because of number one and number two, I didn't make a move.

Until it was too late.

• • •

It's a sunny and windy mid-September day, a few weeks into the fall semester of my sophomore year, and I'm feeling pretty good when I walk into my dorm room. I've been sharing with Darryn Kaneko since our first semester, and we've gotten to be super close since we first got tossed together because we're both on the gymnastics team. Darryn's better than me, but not by much, and sometimes I get the best of him in the gym. Usually on floor exercise.

Darryn gets the best of me this time, because when I

push open the door, he's on his bed. Naked. And decidedly not alone.

I'm frozen at first, stunned by what I'm seeing. It takes my brain a few seconds to work out that the person wrapped around my best friend and super-secret crush is a guy.

"Holy shit! You're *gay*?"

The words burst out of my mouth before I can even think of stopping them, and that's what it takes for the two of them to realize I'm there. Darryn's wide eyes meet my gaze from where he's lying on his back with the guy over him, and he's as frozen as I am for a second before he scrambles to get the sheet pulled up in a vain attempt to cover up what's going on.

"Do you *mind*?" he snaps out. "I put a goddamned note on the door."

His uncharacteristic anger yanks me out of my fugue, and I spin around on my heel so at least I'm not staring anymore. At their naked bodies. Their naked, sweaty, *oh my God my roommate is having gay sex* bodies.

"Jesus *Christ*, Grant. Could you at least wait outside while we put some clothes on?"

Oh shit. Dammit. I fumble for the handle to escape and the next thing I know I'm in the hallway, staring at the door. Right below the room number is our sticker of the University of Atlanta logo, complete with gray-and-blue tornado in the center. And below that is a mess of colorful papers. There's always some new flyer showing up on the door, and I never pay any attention to them anymore. This time, though, next to an ad for some off-campus party this weekend, there's a folded piece of paper attached with a piece of tape. My name is scribbled on it in Darryn's messy handwriting. I reach for it on autopilot and unfold it.

Got company. ;) Give me till 3? And knock before you come in. ~ D

It's actually after 3—I know, because it was a few minutes

before when I left the student union—so I don't know how he thought that part would help. Which makes me wonder, how long have they been making the beast with two backs?

Which brings me back to—how in the hell did I not know he'd be willing to make the beast with two backs with a *guy*?

The realization finally hits me then, and a cold chill runs through me, starting from the chest out. My vision blurs and my knees buckle, and I have to catch myself with both hands against the wall to keep from crumpling to the floor.

Darryn is gay. My best friend, teammate, and roommate. The guy I've been sharing most of my life with for well over a year…and crushing on for most of that time.

Is.

Gay.

And somebody else got to him first.

Fuck. My. Life.

"Hey man, you okay?"

I recognize the voice as Pace Solomon, who lives a few rooms down the hall. I turn my head without removing my forehead from where it's pressed against the wall, because if I do, I might start pounding that spot until I bash my skull open.

"Yeah," I lie. Pace is a nice guy—and hot, too, all piercing eyes and lean muscle and massive thighs from catching for the baseball team—but he tends toward the clueless side sometimes. "Just forgot about something."

Pace doesn't look convinced, but for once he leaves me alone, and that's all I care about. I'm so out of it I don't even take the chance to secretly watch his fine ass as he ambles away. My mind's still stuck on the fine ass of my roommate and the guy he's fucking.

"Argh." I do beat my head against the wall then, though not hard enough to bruise.

The one who's really getting fucked here is me.

The door a foot to my right opens, and the naked-guy-who's-not-my-roommate-and-also-isn't-naked-anymore comes out. The dude gives me a once-over and sneers. "He's all yours," he says, as if he has any claim to my best friend other than the fact that he's been naked in bed with him and I haven't.

"You said it, not me," I spit back.

I don't give him time to come up with a response. I'm inside the room with the door closed behind me and my backpack hurled onto my bed in seconds.

"I'd say I'm sorry you walked in on that, but it's your own fault." Darryn's in boxer-briefs and a tank top, though his skin still glistens with sweat and maybe other bodily fluids. He's standing next to his bed with his hands on his hips, which only serves to show off his massive arm muscles. "I left a note. Like we talked about."

Post-coital Darryn makes for quite the vivid picture, but I won't let myself be distracted right now. "Like we talked about *over a year ago*," I shoot back, waving my arms for emphasis. "When we first moved in together. Not once since then has either of us used it. I had no idea you'd suddenly decided to start bringing back hookups or whatever that was. So no, I didn't see the goddamned note."

I don't even care how mockingly I repeat his words (complete with head tilts). I'm still too busy being pissed off— at him for *being gay, fucking hell*, and at me for not figuring it out until someone else got his hands all over that perfectly sculpted body.

"Well, excuse me for getting some." Darryn stomps over to his closet and starts rummaging through it. Probably looking for the right pair of jeans to show off his bubble butt to all the men on campus who would love to get a piece of it. Me included. "Not my fault if you can't get a date."

Wait, what?

"I cannot *believe* you." I'm in his face before I know I'm moving, even though that puts me halfway in his closet. Poetic. "I've spent every waking hour of the year that I wasn't in class or at home for breaks with *you*. Practice, meals, studying, sleeping in the same room. When, exactly, was I supposed to find a hookup, much less a date?" And that brings me up short. "For that matter, when, exactly, did *you* have time to find one?"

Darryn pushes past me to his bed and starts shoving his legs into his jeans. "We make time for the things that matter."

And I've spent over a year making time for you, I think, though I manage not to say that out loud, at least. "And in all this time you couldn't mention *once* that getting fucked mattered to you? You're supposed to be my best friend."

Darryn's shoulders droop, and he doesn't look at me. "For a best friend," he says, "you sure don't seem to want to be honest with me about who you are."

The words hang between us like he'd shouted them, and the icy ball in my gut sends up a spike that threatens to pierce my throat. "I don't—"

He shakes his head and goes back to fastening his jeans. "I knew you were gay within a month after we met," he says. "I figured eventually you'd trust me enough to tell me."

He might as well have slapped me across the face.

"You didn't tell me, either!" I lash out. "If you're gonna talk about trust, you could have told me."

He finally looks up at me, and the pain in his eyes matches the pain in my heart.

"There wasn't anything to tell," he rasps out. "Not to start with." He yanks a T-shirt over his head and then grabs his keys and phone off his bedside table. "It took another good six months before I figured out that I liked guys, too."

He shoves his feet into flip-flops, grabs his duffel bag from the floor at the end of his bed, and pushes past me.

My heart races the farther away he moves. "How did you know?" The question jumps out of me, and he stops with his hand on the door handle. I can feel the tension in his body from three feet away.

He finally turns his head far enough for me to see his profile, his features etched with pain.

"It took me six months to realize that I was falling for you."

He's out the door and gone then, and my knees finally do give out.

At least my bed is there to catch me.

· · ·

Darryn doesn't come back until late. Late enough that I'm half considering calling everyone I know to find out if they've seen him, and then maybe the campus police if that doesn't pan out.

I've spent the rest of the evening alternating between staring at the wall and pacing the floor, the last few hours running in a loop in my head, but I keep getting stuck on the same thing.

I was falling for you.

How could I be so completely oblivious? Six months. Six months of pining after Darryn, and if I'd ever once gotten my head out of my ass, I might have realized that he felt the same damn way. Might have finally had a chance to do more with a guy than just a few kisses. Might have Darryn in my bed every night, and not only in my dreams.

And now it was too late.

Finally exhausted from pacing and stressing, I threw myself in bed around eleven and proceeded to check the phone every ten minutes. More like every five.

My phone's just finished telling me it's 12:13 a.m.—

and Darryn's always been an early-to-bed type, even on weekends—when the door slowly eases open, like he's trying to sneak in.

Which he is, of course. Because this is how we operate now, apparently. Hiding from each other.

"Don't bother." I get a sick sort of joy from the way he jumps. "I'm awake."

Darryn sighs and tosses his duffel back into its usual spot. "Go to sleep," he grumbles. "We're not talking about this now."

I think I hear him mutter "or ever" under his breath. Like that's gonna happen. I will give him a break tonight, though, only because I know he has a calculus exam coming up that's had him tearing out his hair, almost literally. And even though I'm pissed at him on so many levels it's like a parking garage all up in my brain—level one, anger; level two, hurt; level three, *oh my God, you're gay??*—we're still supposed to be friends.

And that's something I'd like to retain out of whatever else happens, at least.

"Okay. Tomorrow, then." I roll over, putting my back to him and the bed that changed the entire course of my life a few hours earlier. "Good night."

We lie there in silence, neither of us sleeping, until finally we do.

• • •

In the morning, of course, we don't talk. Darryn's up and out the door before I'm awake enough to stop him, and I don't see him again until gym. Where we proceed to ignore the hell out of each other. Because reasons.

Well. I try to ignore him. But my traitorous gaze keeps seeking him out anyway. Does he look different? Happier? Is this guy really what he wants, or is it—

"Clark! You're up!"

Fuck. Worst practice of my career. That's the third time Coach Everson has had to prompt me, and he's pissed as hell about it. I shake my head once, hard, and focus my frustration into the job ahead of me.

I blow out a long breath, bounce onto my toes, and start the long run up to the vault. The empty stands blur in my periphery, and I can tell as I hit the board that I've got it nailed. My hands slam the wide, curved top of the vault, and I punch off with all my strength and pull my arms in tight, twisting my body as I fly through the air.

I hit the mat with my balance a tiny bit off-center, and I have to take a small step to recover, but as I punch my fists into the air, I know it's one of my best efforts. Vault's never been my strength, but the new routine that works in more height and an extra half twist rather than trying to add a flip seems to be doing the trick.

I jog over to get my notes from the assistant coach as Coach Everson sends the next team member down the lane. Coach Sato gives me a nod and a tiny, tiny smile. He's the one who worked up my new vault, and he's got to be feeling good about it.

"Good form," he says, back to all business. "Watch the angle when you hit the vault. Your right hand was too high up, and that put you off at the end." He nods again and pats my flank with the hand not holding his ever-present clipboard. "Take a couple of laps to cool down and hit the showers. You're done for today."

For once, I don't argue. Usually I'm all for more time in the gym, more time on the apparatus, but my head's not in it today. Hell, I'm surprised Coach Everson didn't pull me out of the line for the vault. Not paying attention is a problem with any of the six apparatus, but the vault's particularly dangerous if you aren't laser focused.

I give Coach Sato a nod and head for the track that runs around the perimeter of the gym. In less than a minute, I've settled into a slow, steady jog, and I let my mind wander.

Unfortunately, my eyes do, too, zeroing in on Darryn just as he takes off for his turn on the vault.

His body is a solid, taut line as he runs, legs and arms pumping, and then he launches himself into his routine. He's several steps ahead of me in both difficulty and execution on vault, his best event, though we're even on the others except my own specialty, the floor exercise. I watch as he takes a cartwheel into the launch and backflips onto the vault, the muscles in his arms bunching and flexing as he pushes into the air. He pulls his body straight and flips around twice before planting into the mat, not a wobble or step to be seen.

That's okay. I almost make up for it by tripping over my own feet. I snatch my gaze back from ogling my teammate and concentrate on finishing my run. Well, mostly. My mind takes the opportunity to run even more laps around the same questions. Why did I wait so long to say anything to Darryn? How could I have missed my chance so badly? Have I screwed up so much that I've lost my best friend for good?

I'm not sure I want to know the answer to that last one, which is why I can't exactly blame Darryn for avoiding me the next few days—okay, *hell, yes*, I can blame him. Yeah, I've been in avoidance mode, but I'm not the one who's been staying out every night until after I've given up and fallen asleep.

Not this time.

Thursday night, I stake out our room, determined to have this conversation whether Darryn's ready for it or not.

When he opens the door at a quarter to midnight and sees me sitting on the foot of his bed, he takes half a step back as if to turn around and walk right back out.

"Enough is enough." I point to his desk chair. "Sit your ass down and let's talk."

He's going to say no. I can see it coming. I try a different tactic.

Honesty.

What the hell, right?

"I miss you." It's the God's honest truth, and he knows it. "Whatever else is going on, you're still my best friend. Okay? Can we just...*talk* about this?"

He hovers halfway between yes and no for an eternity before he finally lets out a sigh like he's deflating and kicks the door shut. "All right," he grumbles, dropping his backpack on the floor and his ass into his desk chair. "Talk."

That, of course, is the moment when my natural logorrhea decides to get constipated.

My lips flap uselessly, not forming any words for another eternity, before Darryn rolls his eyes. "Look," he says. "I meant what I said before. When I figured out you were gay, it genuinely did not matter to me. You were a nice guy and a good teammate, and that was all that mattered."

He falls silent, and that's when my words start flowing again. "And then you, what, discovered the *flamboyant* side of life?"

I wince even as I say it, and before he can yell or leave, which is what I deserve, I put up a hand. "Sorry. That was stupid. I just..." I let my hand drop. "When you figured it out, why didn't you say something?"

"What was I supposed to say?" Darryn looks at me then, his dark eyes wide and pained. "You obviously didn't trust me enough to tell me about yourself. And I wouldn't have known where to start."

His words slam like a fist into my stomach. "You think I don't trust you?"

Darryn gives me one of his patented raised eyebrows at

that. "We've been friends for a year, Grant." His words are slow, as if talking to a small child. "And you still haven't told me you're gay. What the hell else am I supposed to think?"

He's gotta be kidding me. "You can't think of any reason an athlete on scholarship to a college in the Deep South might be reluctant to come out?"

"Not *come out*, come out." Darryn waves a hand. "I'm not talking about a *Sports Illustrated* cover here. Or even telling the team or anything. I'm talking about telling *me*." He lays his hand over his chest. "The guy you've been living with for a year. The guy who's supposed to be your best friend."

That one I've thought about long enough that I have an answer. "I was afraid," I admit. "I haven't even told my parents yet. My sister knows. I didn't even have to tell her." Some kind of twin thing, I figured. "The first person I told was a friend in high school I kinda had a crush on. I thought maybe…" I shrug. "It didn't go well."

Darryn's hands curl into fists. "Did he hurt you?"

My heart gives a little leap at his concern. "No. Not…not physically, anyway." I lower my head to my chest and curl my arm across my stomach at the memory. "He called me several choice names and never spoke to me again."

The rawness in my voice must affect Darryn, because in my periphery I can see him shift forward, as if he's moving to hug me. He gives great hugs, even though I've only gotten them in celebration or consolation after great or terrible performances in meets. My skin aches, as if it's pulling away from my body, reaching for Darryn's touch.

But he slides back into his chair, and the ache gives way to a jolt of pain. I bite back a gasp, but I can't stop the full-body flinch.

"I'm sorry you went through that." Darryn's voice rasps like his throat is coated with sandpaper. "I thought you knew me better. If I ever did anything that made you think I'd treat you like that—"

"You didn't. But what makes it *my* job to come out anyway?" The frustration of the last few days wells up, spilling out as my voice rises. "You figured out you were gay—"

"Bi, actually."

I pause for only a second. "Okay. Bi. You still *didn't tell me.*" The words tear at my throat. "Why was it all on *me* to come out? You've had months, and you didn't say a word, either."

He does that one-shoulder shrug again. "You had plenty of chances, too."

"But I didn't *know*!" I'm on my feet then, my heart and head pounding, the bitter taste of adrenaline in my mouth. "As far as I knew, you were straight and an athlete. You know damn good and well how most jocks treat gay guys. Or if they even *think* they might be gay."

"I'm not just any guy, Grant!" Darryn pushes to his feet, too, fists clenched at his sides. "You know me. We've talked about everything."

My shoulders slump as all the fight drains out of me. "Everything except this."

The truth falls into the silence between us.

We keep cycling through the same arguments, getting nowhere. I only wanted to talk and clear the air, get my best friend back, and maybe see if what's-his-face is a permanent fixture or if there's still a chance that we could—

Darryn turns away and picks up his backpack. "I have to get going. I have plans tonight."

My stomach drops like a rock. Guess that answers my question.

"With *him*?" I can't stop the way it sounds like an accusation.

Darryn freezes and carefully doesn't look at me. "His name is Rich. And yes, with him." He hooks his backpack over his shoulder. "Probably gonna have plans with him pretty often."

The "you better start getting used to it" goes unspoken.

I slump down onto my bed, hollowed out, and watch as he walks out the door.

Chapter Two

The next morning, I'm sitting alone at a table in the corner of the dining hall, picking at my scrambled eggs and toast, when a tray slides onto the table across from me. For a half second my heart leaps, thinking it's Darryn, but I look up to find it's Annie. I try not to look too disappointed as I give my twin sister what I'm sure is a half-assed smile.

"You look like someone kicked your puppy and stole your pickup truck."

My smile transforms into a teasing sneer. "You been listening to that country channel on Pandora again?"

Annie rolls her eyes behind her glasses as she pulls her hair up into a messy ponytail. Even though we're twins, we don't look all that much alike. For starters, I'm pretty much covered in freckles while she has only a dusting across her nose. We have the exact same red hair, though, more of an auburn shade than Dad's brighter orange shade.

We don't act that much alike, either. I'm the loudmouthed, gregarious extrovert, while Annie's the reserved, shy introvert who runs a phone and computer repair shop out of her dorm room to earn extra money. In fact, she earned enough last year to pay for a private room this year, and she rarely leaves it except for classes and mealtimes—and most of my gymnastics meets. I don't worry about her. Much. She's probably more well-adjusted than I am, and that's without bringing the mess with Darryn into the mix.

Annie doesn't miss much, though, and I know she sees through my snarky facade. She turns her attention to her bowl of oatmeal, which she's loaded down with dried fruit and brown sugar, the only way she'll eat it. "What happened?"

I don't want to out Darryn. That ship sailed long ago for me—when I told Annie I was gay the night of our eighteenth birthday, her only reaction was an eyeroll and a "duh." I choose my words carefully. "I found out Darryn's dating someone, and I didn't handle it well. He's kind of pissed at me." I shrug. "I guess we're pissed at each other."

Annie takes another bite of her oatmeal, swallows, and washes it down with her orange juice.

"Well," she finally says, "that sucks. And not in a fun way."

I snort, caught off guard. I shouldn't be surprised by her, after nineteen years of living side by side, but every now and then she manages to get one past me.

"Yeah. I have no idea what to do." I don't really expect her to have any suggestions. She's had about as much success dating as I have, which is to say, basically none. "The Curse of the Clarks," we've taken to calling it.

Guess it's struck again.

"Just, I guess, keep being his friend." Annie catches my gaze, and she looks serious for once, none of her usual dry, sometimes biting humor in her eyes. Not that it would matter to me, since I know it's a defense mechanism, but even with me, this is a rarity.

"I mean, you're stuck with him anyway," she goes on,

looking down into her oatmeal as if it holds the secrets of the universe. "Even if you changed rooms, you're still teammates." She shrugs one shoulder. "Might as well be a friend."

I nod and chew my bottom lip, knowing she's right. My chest might go tight at the thought of Darryn spending all his time with someone else, granting his devastating smiles and sharing sweet laughs with another guy, but there's nothing I can do about that now.

Then Annie hits me with the kicker.

"Besides," she says, lifting her head to catch my gaze again, and this time that wicked spark is there. "When his new relationship inevitably falls apart, because *of course* he's really in love with *you*, someone's gotta be there to pick up the pieces. Might as well be you, right?"

I bark out a laugh at that. "You are an evil, evil woman." I grin at her and lift my coffee cup in a toast, feeling the least little bit better. "I knew there was something I liked about you."

That gets a glare. "Better watch out. You don't want to end up on the wrong side of my brilliance." Her smile is sickly sweet. "You wouldn't like me when I'm angry."

There's a reason she has a whole collection of T-shirts featuring The Hulk.

· · ·

Classes drag like someone hit the wrong setting on the space-time continuum. I don't know what the problem is. Maybe it's because we have a mock meet in the afternoon. I'll be seeing Darryn but probably won't have a chance to talk to him. Though after the way our last talk went, not talking is probably for the best.

As I cross to the gym after my last class finally lets out,

I give myself a mental pep talk. *Be a friend. Be a teammate. Congratulate him when he does well. Treat him like you would have a week ago.*

By the time I push through the doors of the building that's my second home on campus, I'm feeling pretty good. A couple of guys are out on the floor already, under the watchful eyes of our coaches as they warm up or try out some new moves. I watch one of the freshmen—Kenny, I think his name is—as he works on his Thomas flairs. The floor exercise move, which was invented for the pommel horse by one of my childhood idols, former US Olympian Kurt Thomas, involves swinging wide-spread legs high over the mat and requires strong wrists and great balance.

It's also one of my specialties. Maybe I'll have a talk with the kid, see if I can help with his technique.

My mind is on Kenny and not where I'm going as I hit the locker room door, which explains how I end up chest to chest with my roommate.

Darryn grabs one of my arms to keep us both from falling over. He's already in his uniform, the standard tight tank top and body-hugging pants, and my first instinct is to get my hands and maybe my mouth all over the exposed muscles of his shoulders and arms.

Then my brain catches up to my hormones, and I manage to step away from Darryn without doing anything stupid.

"Sorry." I try to smile. "Million miles away. See you out there."

Darryn hesitates for a moment before he nods and returns my attempt at a smile. The door swings shut behind him, and I walk on autopilot over to my locker to get changed.

Well. Isn't *this* going to be a buttload of fun?

By sheer force of will, I force the whole situation with Darryn out of my mind and focus on practice.

Halfway through our mock meet, I'm feeling pretty good.

We're divided into two teams and do the apparatus rotations, like we would during a regular meet. I nailed my vault with only a slight bobble, and my rings performance was one of my best, even though I know I need to increase the difficulty level if I ever want to reach the top tier in the all-around.

I'm waiting for my turn on the floor now. Technically, I'm rated second on floor exercise to one of the seniors, but he's on the other team today, so I'll be last to perform in our group.

Men's gymnastics doesn't get as much coverage as women's overall, probably because they're very different sports in a lot of ways. The men's performances focus on strength and precision, while women's are heavier on artistry and grace. We share only two apparatus, vault and floor exercise, and men perform in six different categories to women's four. Not to say that men's gymnastics is better than women's or anything like that. They're both tough as hell.

Collegiate gymnastics is a whole different world from the Olympics, too. The number of men's teams is in the teens—and ours is only a few years old—and the women have only a couple dozen. Most of the elite competitors focus on the Olympics, though, which doesn't leave as much talent for the college level.

Heath finishes up his routine and walks off the floor. He's a junior who's done well in his meets, but he takes forever to learn a new move. If he doesn't step things up a notch, the younger guys are going to blow right past him—like I already have.

I glance over to Coach Sato and get the nod that sends me striding out to the center of the mat. I wait for the low buzzer that signals the start of my minute-long routine. I nail the first tumbling pass, which is the toughest of my four, and my round of Thomas flairs flies so high my hands nearly lift off the mat. As I go into my fourth tumbling pass, my heart pumping and my body buzzing, I feel like an Olympic champion about to nail down the gold. Never mind that I'll likely never reach those heights. When I'm on, I can feel it down into my bones. And I'm on today.

I bounce off the mat into my last double backflip, and my feet slam into the mat, sticking the landing. I shoot my arms up over my head into a *V* that means victory. A whoop comes from somewhere off to my left, in a voice that sounds an awful lot like Darryn's, and a grin erupts on my face.

No matter what else is going on in my life, I can always count on gymnastics to be there for me. And I guess, despite everything, I can always count on Darryn to cheer me on.

The way my heart lifts, I don't know which thought comforts me more.

I head off the floor and join my teammates in our rotation to the next apparatus. From across the way, I happen to catch Darryn's gaze as he follows his team over to the vault. He gives me a smile and a wink, and my grin widens.

He still has my back. And knowing that makes everything else fade into the background.

• • •

After I finish my last apparatus, the high bar, Coach Sato calls me aside to offer a few tips on getting my last release move higher. I'm supposed to fly three or four feet above the bar, which is already over eight feet above the ground. Coach and I talk for a while before he suggests I give it a few more tries.

My arms feel like overcooked spaghetti after the hard-driving work of the mock meet, but it's going to take a lot more than that for me to tell any coach no. I cross to the bar, pausing to re-dust my hands with chalk, and then Coach steps behind me to lift me up. Since I'm not doing the full routine, there's no need for me to do a formal mount.

I get a good grasp on the bar before I start swinging. By the time I've worked up to three times around backward, I feel I have enough momentum to give it a try.

The move is called a Yamawaki, named for a Japanese gymnast from the eighties. It's not the most complex in the book, consisting of releasing the bar from a backward swing and taking a half-turn in the air to re-grip the bar facing forward. It's a basic of the sport, though, and the higher you fly, the higher your score.

My first attempt probably hits that three-foot threshold we're looking for, but I almost miss the bar on the way down and have to slow to a stop to get my hands back on solidly.

"Good height," Coach Sato tells me. "A little too far out in front. See if you can push that momentum up instead of out."

I nod and let my body hang for a few seconds before I kick out to start a new swing. This time, everything feels perfect. My hands are secure, my legs are angled just right, and when I push into the release, I feel like I've taken flight.

I come back down in the right spot, grabbing the bar without breaking the flow of my swing. I grin as I take another full swing.

"All right!" I hear Coach yell. "Gimme another one!"

I manage two more, and though the second is still the cleanest of them all, the last two are almost as smooth. I finally bring myself to a stop, arms and wrists screaming at me, and open my hands to drop softly to the mat below.

Movement to my left catches my eye, and I glance that way in time to see a dark-haired figure slipping out the door. I'd know the lines of that body anywhere.

Why did Darryn hang around to watch?

Dammit. Don't tell me he was looking to talk to me after practice and I missed another chance. Why is it that life seems to be conspiring against me?

Well. Nothing I can do about it now. I shake it off and turn my attention back to Coach Sato, who's making a couple more suggestions but then tells me I've done great and sends me off to the showers. My arms are trembling from the extra exertion, and once I'm in the locker room, my fingers don't want to cooperate. I fumble my practice gear off and drop it on a bench before walking into the showers and turning the water on almost too hot to stand. I let it pound down on my sore shoulders and over my arms, soothing the burning muscles even as my pale skin turns bright pink from the heat.

My mind wanders, and I picture Darryn coming back into the locker room, stripping out of his clothes, and following me into the showers. I can almost feel his body behind mine, his arms wrapping around me, his hips notching into place against my ass. My cock throbs, and it's all I can do to yank myself out of the fantasy and not jerk off right there.

I flip the water over to cold and stay under the icy spray until I'm shivering and my balls are crawling into my abdomen. Only then do I dare to turn the shower off and head back into my life.

· · ·

It's after eight when I get back to the dorm. I stopped by the dining hall and grabbed a sandwich after I finished at the gym, but I didn't feel like company. Instead, I found an empty bench in one corner of the quad and sat there to eat. I tried to read the next chapter in my physiology book—why the heck we have to learn about "the integumentary system" instead of "skin" is beyond me—but I couldn't concentrate. I ended up staring off into space for a good twenty minutes thinking about Darryn and how to bridge the chasm between us, before I got sick of my own melancholia and headed back to the room.

Darryn's not there—and yes, I damn well checked the door for a note this time—and his backpack's not in its usual spot by his desk, so I figure he's at the library. *Or at Rich's,* my traitorous mind supplies, and I trip over my own feet as I go to set down my backpack.

Fuck. I have *got* to get past this. No, I'm not gonna get over being in love with Darryn any time soon. Not when I'm still around him all the damn time. I've got to learn to keep my emotions in check. Treat him like a friend and teammate, not like the guy I'm pining for.

Even if that's exactly what I'm doing. All the time.

I need a distraction. Practice helps, but I can't separate things completely because, no matter how focused I am, Darryn's always there. School may do it some of the time, but this evening's reading fail shows it's not going to be enough. I could go out and find a guy of my own, but that would just look like sour grapes.

Besides, I'm not ready for that anyway.

A memory floats back from practice earlier in the week—that kid Kenny working on his flairs. Maybe I can talk to Coach Everson about helping him out sometime. I can always use the extra work, and it'd be good practice, especially if I decide to get into coaching eventually.

It's a good plan. I can work toward my goal, it means more time in the gym, and it'll keep my mind off Darryn.

All right, then. I'll do it.

I feel a little better having made that decision. Now all I can do is hope that it's enough to do the trick.

Unfortunately, my grand *find a distraction and don't mope about Darryn* plan has to be put on hold until I get the chance to talk to Coach Everson. He's MIA from practice one day, and the next he has us split up into groups, each working with a different apparatus. I'm on rings, definitely my weakest of the six disciplines, and after a grueling two hours spent taking my turns holding myself steady with my arms straight out to the sides—the Iron Cross should be registered as medieval torture—I'm too wiped to think about anything other than a shower. Maybe I should work myself into exhaustion every day. It shuts my brain down pretty well, and I get the best night's sleep I've had in over a week.

Doesn't stop me from waking up thinking about Darryn.

That afternoon, I manage to get to the gym early enough to catch Coach Everson before he leaves his office. I knock on the jamb of the open door, and Coach glances up, then lifts an eyebrow before he waves me in.

"Clark." His voice is neutral. "Can I help you with something?"

"I was thinking…" *That maybe I should've planned what I was going to say first, dammit.* "I mean, I saw you working with Washington—I mean, Kenny—on his flairs on the floor earlier in the week. I thought maybe I could work with him a little on that. Give him some tips and get some coaching practice at the same time."

It's not the smoothest speech ever, but it gets the point across. Coach must think so, too, because he's nodding by the time I'm done.

"That could work." He tilts his head. "It's not going to affect your schoolwork?"

I shake my head. "I'm doing fine. I can handle it." My classes right now are mostly boring and not all that difficult. I'm not a straight-A student like Annie, but I hold my own.

"Okay, then. I'll talk to Niko"—Coach Sato— "and Kenny about it, see what they think. Let you know what we decide."

I nod quickly. "Thanks. I'll just…" I point. "Go get changed."

Smooth, Clark.

I spin on my heel and book it down the hall to the locker room before I embarrass myself any more.

• • •

Among the perks of no longer being a freshman is that I have more flexibility about my schedule, so I have only one class on Fridays, and it's not until eleven. Darryn's schedule is the same, though the class is different, so we've taken to sleeping in until the last possible second and then scrambling into whatever clothes we can find and running across campus.

The freedom to sleep in also means that I'm always up late on Thursday nights, watching whatever's hot on Netflix or surfing the internet aimlessly. It's well after midnight and I've just finished a ridiculously bad disaster flick—Annie and I have been trying to one-up each other by finding the very worst ones for years—when the door handle turns and Darryn slips quietly into the room.

"Don't bother," I say, doing my best to sound teasing and not like an accusation. "I'm still up."

Darryn snorts and drops his backpack in its usual spot. "You didn't need to wait up for me, *Dad*. I was only a couple of blocks away."

I open my mouth to make a comment about the dad thing when his words sink in. I thought he'd been at the library. "You were with Rich?"

That *does* sound accusatory, and Darryn recoils like I'd slapped him.

"Yes, I was with *my boyfriend*," he grits out through clenched teeth. "You have a problem with that?"

It takes every drop of willpower in every fiber of my being not to tell him the truth. "No," I finally force out. "Sorry. I just... I thought you were at the library."

I kind of mumble the last of it into the thick tension filling the room. It's a lame excuse, considering the library closed nearly an hour ago. Eventually, Darryn turns toward his closet.

"I'm headed to the showers," he throws back over his shoulder. "I don't want to fight with you."

His shoulders slump, and I want nothing in the world more than to go to him. Comfort him. But that's not my job. It never was. And if I don't keep my yap shut and leave him alone about this, there's not a chance in hell it ever could be.

"I don't want to fight, either." I close my laptop and push it aside. "I'm trying. I was surprised, okay? I need a little time to adjust."

Darryn nods, but he still doesn't turn to face me. "I get that. I do."

He doesn't say anything more, just grabs his towel and shower caddy and heads for the bathroom across the hall. I watch the door fall shut behind him and stare at the bare wood until my eyes start to burn.

Dammit. I climb off the bed, move my laptop to my desk, and then strip down to my boxer-briefs and crawl under the covers. Curled up on my side, my back to Darryn's bed, I close my eyes and try to will myself to fall asleep before he comes back.

Sometimes outright avoidance is the greater part of valor.

· · ·

Avoidance seems to be Darryn's plan, too. He's up and gone before I even wake up on Friday, and he doesn't reappear after class, when we usually grab lunch in the student union before heading to the gym. I go through my usual routine anyway, trying to keep my mind on my workout and decidedly off my MIA best friend.

We don't do a lot of weightlifting as part of our training—

muscle injury can be a huge problem—but I know I need to get my shoulders and arms stronger if I want to up my game on the rings. When I walk into the weight room, I'm happy to see I've got the place to myself. I know it won't last, but I'm sure as hell going to take advantage.

After a warmup on the elliptical, I settle into the biceps machine and start curling. I'm working slow and steady, increasing the weight by ten pounds after every set of ten reps, when the door across the room opens and Pace Solomon walks in.

"Hey." I nod my acknowledgment.

"Hey." He does the same as he crosses to the same elliptical machine I used. "Arms day?"

It's a silly question, considering what I'm doing. "Yeah. Need to work on my shoulders for rings."

Pace gives a small laugh and shakes his head, then climbs onto the machine. "That stuff where you have to hold yourself up like you're on a cross? Damn, man. That's gotta hurt."

I snort and bend down to increase the weight again. "You don't know the half of it."

I go back to my biceps curls while Pace gets started on his warmup. We work in silence except for harsh breathing and a grunt or two for the next five minutes, until the timer on Pace's machine sounds and he slows to a stop. He climbs down and grabs the towel he brought with him to wipe his face and neck—he wasn't working that hard, but he had a sweat going anyway—and then heads my way.

"You close to done?" he asks. "'Cause I can start with lats if you aren't."

My arms are starting to shake, so I give him a nod. "Four more."

I power through the last four curls and lower the weight back into place, then lean back and shake out both arms.

"Burning?" Pace asks.

I bark out a quick laugh. "Feels like victory!"

I slide off the machine and grab my towel to give it a quick wipe-down. Pace nods his thanks and takes my place while I move to the butterfly machine. We're both on our second round of reps before he speaks again.

"So," he says, arms curling in perfect form. I try not to watch the muscles bulging too closely. Hey, he's a hot guy; what can I say?

"Haven't seen your boy around much lately." Pace's words take a few seconds to sink in. *My boy.* Not so much.

"You mean Darryn?" I'm proud of myself for not choking on the name. "He's been busy. Personal stuff. Nothing bad."

Well, it's true, as far at that goes. I'm not about to out him without his permission, and "dating someone" would only draw more questions.

"Oh, okay." Pace pauses to increase his weight. "That guy he was with the other day? He a friend of yours?"

That gets my attention. "What guy?" I ask carefully.

Pace shrugs and slides his arms back into the curl bars. "Big. Kinda muscley. Shaved head. Looked like he was mad about something."

I take in a breath and blow it out carefully. "No, not a friend of mine. Friend of Darryn's. I only met him once."

Jesus Christ, this is like navigating a mine field. Why did Pace have to go and get conversational *now*, of all times?

"Oh. Just wondering. Thought I saw him in the dorm a couple of weeks ago. He looked mad then, too."

Probably because he didn't get his rocks off. I shrug as I lean over to adjust the weights. "Maybe. That's about when I met him."

I focus on my workout then, hoping Pace will do the same—or, at least, stop asking me questions about Darryn. We make it through our rounds on those machines, and I'm halfway through my lat workout before Pace pipes up again.

"Don't you and Darryn usually work out together?"

Fuck this. I let the weight clang down and swing around to stare at Pace.

"Why the hell do you suddenly care? You wanna get me out of the picture so you can get in his pants or something?"

Fuckity *fuck.* The words aren't even out of my mouth before I regret them. "Sorry!" I choke out, holding up one hand, palm out. I'm apologizing a lot lately. "That was totally out of bounds. And homophobic. And ridiculous on about eight different levels." I take another cleansing breath and let my arm drop to my side. "Seriously, though. Darryn and I aren't joined at the hip." *At least not this semester.* "He's doing some things on his own right now." *Things I wish he was doing with me and not some other guy.* "It's no big deal." *It's only turned my entire life upside down.*

Pace's eyes are wide, and I'm betting he has about a billion more questions now than he ever did before. He might be a little slow on the uptake sometimes, but he's not stupid. He gives a short nod and goes back to his workout.

Fifteen minutes later, I finish up and climb off the last machine. I'm giving it the usual wipe-down when Pace speaks up again.

"So, uh." He clears his throat. "If you wanna... Maybe we could work out together sometimes? I could use some spotting on a couple of the machines when I'm working core, at least. If you're not working out with D... With someone else."

I don't have a good reason to turn him down, and workouts do seem to go faster when you're with someone else. "That might work," I tell him. "Look for me in the dorm later and we'll set something up."

"Great!" Pace smiles his Hollywood-perfect smile, and despite myself, I flush. Damn, he is one fine-looking man. My heart might belong to Darryn, but that doesn't stop my hormones from reacting to someone as gorgeous as Pace.

My hormones are just going to have to get over it. I do my best to return Pace's smile and then head to the locker room. Where I will *not* think about Darryn while I'm in the shower, dammit.

Chapter Three

A door slamming down the hall jerks me awake in the middle of the night, and my neck screams a protest at the movement. I wince and rub the sore muscles from where I fell asleep propped up on my side, my laptop running Netflix in front of me. The screen is asking if I'm still there, and I reach over to click out of the system. I'll have to go back later to figure out where I left off. My plan had been a binge re-watch of *Stranger Things*, but the last bit I remember was the opening scene of the fourth episode.

I roll onto my back and stretch my whole body before glancing over at the bedside clock, which glows a red 2:13. My brain finally catches up, and I sit up and stare over at Darryn's side of the room.

Empty bed. No backpack. No sign that he's been here at all.

My stomach twists at the implications, and I have to push back the urge to grab my phone and text to find out where he is. He's a grown man. He can stay out late if he wants to.

Or stay out all night, for that matter.

With his boyfriend.

Just like that, the pile of Cheez-Its I scarfed while Netflixing threatens to make a reappearance. I swallow down the bile and swing my legs over the side of the bed to prop my elbows on my knees and scrub my palms over my eyes. I've got to quit acting like I have a reason to be angry about this. It's my own damn fault for not speaking up.

It's my own damn fault I let him get away.

My skin feels too small for my body, tight and itchy, and the walls are closing in around me. I can't lie back down and stare at the ceiling until morning and do nothing but replay my entire relationship with Darryn and how not once did I find the courage to tell him how I feel.

Enough.

I stand up and yank open the top drawer of my dresser to pull out a pair of socks, shove my feet into them, and then put on my sneakers and a hoodie. I grab my cell phone off the charger and jam my keys into my pocket on my way out the door.

It feels like every tight muscle in my body relaxes when I step outside. The dark, cool night soothes me, the fresh air washing over my skin like a smooth dive into a clear lake. It's a nice campus, all green spaces and curved, lighted sidewalks, and I see a few other students wandering around, mostly in pairs. I ignore the handholding and faces too close together to be "just friends" and instead turn my attention to the sky high above. Stars are hard to pick out even on a good night this close to the city, and tonight the moon is near full, the added brightness overpowering the dimmer points of light.

I stop at a bench near the library and sit down, hands shoved deep into my jacket pockets and my head tilted back. Eyes closed, I listen to the breeze ruffling through the leaves in the trees, the soft trills of frogs in the pond nearby, and the distant sounds of traffic along the road at the mouth of the campus.

My mind settles, and I'm the calmest I've been in weeks. I've almost forgotten what it feels like.

It doesn't last long. Soon I hear voices approaching, the chatter and laughter of a group of girls—women, I suppose, since they're college students. They pass me by, throwing glances my way but not stopping, and somehow the way they act, like it's not weird for me to be sitting alone out here in the middle of the night, washes away the last of my disquiet.

Yeah, okay, I might be an adult, legally speaking. But I'm still a teenager for a few more months, at least. I know all about adolescent hormones and the kind of havoc they can wreak even when things are going well. Throw in the kind of turmoil I've been dealing with, and even though I spend half the time feeling like I'm about to lose it, I'm practically a poster boy for mental health stability.

I don't know if that's enough to help me sleep at night, but it's a start.

I push to my feet and walk some more, eventually making a round of the entire campus. I've never measured the distance or counted the steps. I'd guess it's a mile and a half all told. By the time I get back to the dorm, exhaustion is settling into my bones, and it's all I can do to drag myself up to the second floor and down the hall to the room. Once inside, I shuffle to my bed, dropping my shoes and hoodie on the floor and my keys and phone on my bedside table.

I crawl back onto the mattress, curling up against my pillow, my brain silent for once. Not empty—Darryn's still there, like always. But it's a quiet presence, the knowledge that he's still in my life, and that I'm lucky to have him.

Within minutes, I'm dead to the world.

• • •

Saturday passes with no word from Darryn. At midafternoon, I convince myself that his disappearing without a word gives me enough reason to send him a quick text. I stick to *everything ok?* and get a reply an hour later: *yeah, sorry, be back late tomorrow.* No word about where he is or what (*who*) he's doing, but I'm not his keeper, right?

I spend Sunday mostly in the library. I have a tendency to let my schoolwork slide until the weekend—or until the night before an exam—so I spend a lot of the Saturdays and Sundays when we don't have meets camped out in a carrel, catching up on reading and assignments. Probably not the most efficient way of doing things, but it's worked okay to this point. Anyway, my grades are good enough to keep my coaches and my parents satisfied—and it's no mistake that they're ranked in that order of importance.

I lose track of time until my stomach grumbles at me and I check my phone to find it's almost seven. I haven't eaten since I grabbed a muffin and coffee at the dining hall around eleven, and if I don't hurry, there won't be anything edible left for dinner but liver and onions or the equivalent.

After shoving my stuff into my backpack, I head outside and around the corner toward the student union building. Thunder rumbles overhead, a late summer storm threatening, and I reach the door as the first few raindrops fall.

The dining hall is nearly empty, normal for a Saturday evening. Half the students here commute from off campus anyway, and the ones who live in the dorms usually have better things to do on Saturday nights. Hell, I've certainly been to my share of parties in the houses nearby that are rented out to students. I probably could still find one, but all I want to do right now is eat something, go back to the room, and veg in front of a screen.

Pathetic, that's what I am.

A memory pops up then, of a party I'd dragged Darryn

to early in the semester. The house was only two blocks away from the campus, near enough to walk, rented out by several juniors who were celebrating their newfound off-campus freedom with a blowout celebration. I knew one of the guys from my psych class, but not his roommates. I still couldn't tell you their names. I can remember what they looked like from when Boyd introduced me, though.

One of them was Rich.

Which means, as if it's not bad enough that I blew my own chance with him, I actually created the opportunity for Darryn to meet the bastard in the first place.

Well, that's one way to kill my appetite.

I force myself to get food anyway. If I don't, I'll be nauseated and starving later. The food here is decent, the kitchen's apparent obsession with liver and onions aside, but they shut down at eight on Saturday nights, which means it can be slim pickings this late. I get a thick slice of meatloaf with mashed potatoes and corn on the side, none of which looks appetizing in the least. At least it's relatively bland.

I turn to look for a table and almost run into someone with my tray.

"Surprise!" Annie sticks her tongue out at me. "Up for company?"

I shrug one shoulder as my heart rate settles back down to normal. "Don't know how good I'll be, but sure." I nod behind me. "Better get while the gettin's good."

Annie glances toward the glass front of the building, where I can see rain coming down in sheets outside. "Maybe find a table in the corner?" Away from the windows, she means. Lightning flashes, making her flinch. I love a good electrical storm, but they've never been Annie's favorite thing.

"Will do." I head toward the seating area farthest from the windows, and when I pick a table, I slide into the side facing out. Best of both worlds. I can watch the light show while Annie can keep her back to it and pretend it isn't happening.

Annie comes over a few minutes later with a tray that's identical to mine, right down to the glass of tea. She sends me a brief look of gratitude for my seating choice as she slides into the chair across from me. Thunder cracks overhead, and she flinches again.

"Dammit." She stabs her fork into her meatloaf. I know her fear of storms bothers her, even though I've tried to tell her it's a perfectly rational thing to be afraid of. It never gets through, though, so I go for distraction instead.

"You'll never guess who I worked out with yesterday afternoon."

Annie rolls her eyes. "I'm assuming not your roommate, or you wouldn't be making a pronouncement about it."

I'm pretty proud that I don't flinch myself at the mention of Darryn. "None other than Pace Solomon, rising star of the University of Atlanta Tornadoes baseball team and the hottest thing on two legs."

"Doesn't ring a bell." She sounds cool and collected. As usual, I see right through that.

"Ah ah ah." I wave a scolding finger. "I know you better than that. Don't think I've forgotten how you had your butt planted in the stands for every home game last spring. Or whose tight little butt and pretty green eyes kept you coming back for more."

She slumps in her seat. "I love baseball," she defends, weakly. "You know that."

"That's why you went to the *first* game," I shoot back. "Not what kept you going back."

If it's possible to chew resentfully, Annie manages it. I just grin. "Anyway, turns out Pace is a pretty cool dude. Down-to-earth and all that. Doesn't lord his iridescent beauty over us lesser mortals."

Annie almost chokes on her snort. She pauses to swallow and take a sip of her drink. "Iridescent?" she parrots. "He's not a sparklepire, dorkwad."

"Watch out, Annieconda, or I'll tell him about your secret love for all things Cullen."

A shudder runs through her. "Still can't believe I read those things. I want that brain space back. Someone should invent a memory eraser that targets bad books and movies."

"And music," I add. "Can you imagine how great it would be to excise all the Nickelback riffs from your brain?"

Annie immediately starts humming one of them—I have no idea which song, they all run together anyway—and I respond by flicking a kernel of corn at her. She actually giggles at that, and I laugh in response, because I know that means I've won.

"Anyway," Annie says when we stop laughing. "If you think Pace is such perfection, why aren't you going after him? I mean, sure, I think he's gorgeous, but I'm never going to actually date someone like that."

I give her an eyebrow. "Hey now. No putting yourself down. You know that's my job."

"Jerkwad." She tosses my rogue corn kernel back at me, but something in her expression has me paying closer attention. "Besides…"

I wait for her to go on, then finally prod her foot with my toe. "Besides what?"

Annie sighs and looks down at the deconstructed remains of her meatloaf. "I think I might kinda…likegirlstoo?"

It takes me a second to untangle the words. And *whoa.* "Any, um." I clear my throat, determined to be as cool about this as she was when I came out to her. "Any particular girls?"

She pokes her mashed potatoes with her fork. "Well, I like baseball…and I kinda like softball, too."

Her cheeks are flushed bright pink, half hidden by the fall of her hair, and I fight the urge to reach over and brush the long strands out of the way. "That's cool," I say instead. "I mean, I like guys, but that doesn't mean I can't appreciate a beautiful woman." I nudge her foot again. "You need any help snagging one of them, let me know."

Annie snorts and glances up, a more normal-looking smirk on her face. "Yeah, like I'm going to you for relationship advice. Even theoretical."

I do flinch then, and there's no hiding my reaction. "Yeah, well, about that."

Annie sits up straighter. "Did he break up with the chick?"

My laugh is as hollow as my heart. "Oh no. It's *way* worse than that." I sure can't talk about it here, though. I crumple up my napkin and drop it on my plate. "Let's get out of here."

An hour later, we're in Annie's dorm room, an open bag of miniature Reese's peanut butter cups and two bottles of root beer between us on her bed. After we left the dining hall, Annie dragged me through the fading drizzle down to the overpriced snack shop in the student union for provisions. I've just finished vomiting up the rest of the story—and possibly parts of my spleen—and I unwrap two more Reese's cups, and pop both into my mouth to chew listlessly. I know outing Darryn without his permission is kind of a dick move, but my whole friendship with Darryn is in tatters, and I need *someone* to talk to about what I've been dealing with. Besides, Annie's not going to tell anyone.

Annie takes a sip from her bottle. "Well," she finally says. "At least you don't have to wonder if he likes guys anymore."

I snort. "Fat lot of good it does me."

"For now." Annie grabs another peanut butter cup. "I mean, what are the odds this Rich dude is gonna last? Especially since Darryn said he's in love with you."

"Was," I correct. "*Was* in love."

Annie shrugs. "Didn't hear anything in what you told me that sounded like he'd fallen *out* of love."

She watches me as she eats her Reese's cup, and I can just imagine the startled expression on my face. She's right. Maybe it's a thin straw to grasp, but Darryn said he'd fallen in love with me. He did *not* say he didn't still love me, and he *damn* sure didn't say he was in love with Rich.

A tiny warmth flickers to life deep in my chest.

If I had to give it a name, I'd call it hope.

• • •

As promised, Darryn shows up back in our room late Sunday afternoon, looking tired and lugging a duffel bag. "Hey," he says, dropping his backpack in its usual spot and lifting the duffel onto his desk.

"Hey," is my brilliant reply. I watch as he opens the bag and starts pulling out dirty clothes and tossing them into the basket in the bottom of his closet. Which means he didn't spend the weekend at his parents'. My heart sinks at the realization.

"Did you get that paper done for English lit?"

I nod absently, still staring at the evidence proving Darryn's been with Rich the past two days. Probably fucking. And *that's* a mental image I could really use Annie's hypothetical memory eraser for.

"Grant? You in there?"

I snap back to attention to find Darryn staring at me, an expression halfway between annoyance and amusement on his face. "Sorry," I blurt out. "Didn't sleep well last night."

It's the truth, at least. I finished the series I'd been watching on Netflix and started another, and it had to be close to sunrise before I finally dozed off. Loud voices in the hallway woke me a few minutes after ten, so I couldn't have gotten more than about five hours.

Darryn doesn't look as though he believes me, but he lets it go. "Anyway, I have the thing mostly written out. I just need to type it up." He's talking about the lit paper, right. "I probably won't have time to go to the dining hall, so I thought I'd spring for pizza from Charlie's…if you want to share?"

Charlie's pizza with Darryn. It's been a monthly tradition practically since we met, sometimes at the restaurant and sometimes in the room, and a part of me wants to jump at the chance for a slice of normalcy. Even though it's totally different now because he knows I've got a thing for him, and regardless of whether he might return my feelings, he's dating someone else. Which means he's totally off-limits.

And you've got to learn to live with that, I remind myself.

"Sounds great." I try to smile. "I've still got to read a chapter for anthropology anyway."

Darryn smiles, and it almost feels like it did before.

Almost.

• • •

A shrill whistle cuts the air as I step into the gym, ten minutes early for practice, which to the coaches is five minutes late. Guys are spread out all over the mats in various stages of warmups, but all heads pop up at the noise and swivel toward Coach Everson.

"Coach Sato's running practice today," he announces. "I'll be observing. I know you know this, but you listen to him like you would me. Got it?"

All those heads nod, and I start back toward the locker room to get changed. "Clark!" Everson yells. I pause and turn his way. "Get changed and come find me."

I nod again and push into the locker room. I rush through changing into my practice gear and give a few short stretches before heading back out. Back in the gym, I search out Coach Everson where he's standing off to one side, talking with Kenny.

Oh. Right. I said I'd help train the kid. Guess that's starting today.

I cross over to the two of them and shoot Kenny a quick smile. "Hey. Ready to get started?"

Coach Everson claps me on the shoulder in some display of support or warning or, I don't know, heteronormative machismo. "Clark here is one of our strongest on flairs. You pay close attention and we'll get you where you need to be."

Kenny nods, eyes wide with the earnest look all the freshmen have when they get a little personal attention from the head coach. I know I wore the same expression more often than not during my first few months on the team.

"C'mon." I wave the kid toward one of the practice mats, which is clear now that the rest of the team has headed off to work on the full apparatus. This mat is about a third the size of the official floor exercise mat, but it's made of the same springy material, designed for the kind of specialized work we'll be doing.

I haven't put all that much thought into how to show Kenny what he needs to be doing to get his flairs where they need to be. I know he can do the moves, just from watching him during practices on the floor, pommel horse, and parallel bars. It's the same progression either way, the only difference is having your hands planted flat on the mat for the floor instead of gripping the pommels or bars.

"Okay," I start. "Let's see you go at it."

Kenny blows out a breath as he lowers himself to the mat. He works his way into the flairs carefully, until he's got his legs swinging smoothly and his arms working with precision. I watch him closely, seeing a hitch in his motion when he picks up his left arm and moves it to the other side of his leg. Aha. Bet that's what's holding him back.

I stop him and point out the problem. Turns out he had a shoulder injury a couple of years earlier, and while it rarely bothers him anymore, he didn't realize he's still favoring that side. He concentrates on that for a few minutes, and while he still has a ways to go, he's doing much better already.

"Great job!" If I'm going to play coach, I've got to remember to give some praise along with the correction, right?

Kenny grins widely as he comes to rest on the mat. "Would you…I don't know, demonstrate?" He's stumbling over his words, and it might be cute if he were my type. Darryn's face flashes in my mind, and I have to physically stop myself from looking around to find him wherever he is across the floor.

"Sure." Kenny scrambles to the side, and I swing into action, letting my body take over as I spin into the rotation. When I have the momentum going, I shift into the flairs, swapping my hands around my legs and swinging my legs up high toward the ceiling. One of the reasons I've gotten so good at this move is that it feels like I'm about to take flight every time. Like one good push at precisely the right angle and I'll be soaring high above the floor.

Okay, well, technically that does happen on horse and bars, but it's not the same thing.

I bring myself back down from the flairs, swiveling into a split, and glance over at Kenny. The expression on his face has shifted. He still looks eager, all right, but it's not learning he's interested in.

Well, shit.

I smother a sigh. I guess a student crush is one of the many things I'll have to learn about coaching if that's what I end up doing. I give Kenny a short smile and a nod as I move out of the way.

"Give it another shot." I do my best to keep my voice firm and businesslike. "Remember to point your toes and concentrate on stretching out your legs. The long lines will make the flairs look bigger even if you're not getting full extension off the floor."

Kenny moves even faster this time to follow my instructions. I don't know that his flairs are any better than they were a few minutes ago, but at least his interest is keeping him, well, interested.

We work for another ten minutes before Coach Sato stops next to us. "Okay, time's up for the private lessons, guys. Washington, head over to the vault. Clark, you're up on rings."

Great, my favorite. I don't smother the sigh this time as I clamber up and give Kenny a quick wave before jogging over to stare down the rings. *We meet again,* I think—and have to bite back a crazy giggle before it sneaks out.

Coach Sato comes up behind me. "Okay, let's work on your swings," he says. "Concentrate on keeping the rings still." That's their name, after all—still rings. The point is to keep them from moving, especially when holding strength poses like crosses. The less movement during the full-body swings that are part of the routine requirements, the easier it is to keep the rings motionless in between.

Easier said than done, that's for sure.

I follow Coach's instructions as I work, taking breaks for other teammates to take their turns. My arms and shoulders are burning like fire when we finish—the good burn from muscles worked hard, not the true pain that would come from an injury.

Coach ends our session with a clap of his hands. "Great work, guys. Hit the showers and I'll see you tomorrow."

The four of us make a beeline for the locker room, where another group is right ahead of us. There are twenty of us total on the team, most on some kind of athletic scholarship. Between the state HOPE scholarship from the lottery and the school's own financial support programs, tuition and books are covered for most students anyway. Scholarships are used to cover housing and food. That means, thanks to the requirement that freshman and sophomores in all sports live on campus, I've got pretty much a full ride through the end of the year.

I follow my teammates into the locker room and strip down quickly before heading to the shower, eager to get some hot water on my aching muscles. I'm not so eager to be naked in the same space as Darryn, but hell, it's not like none of us has ever sprouted wood in the locker room before. Sexuality aside, the potent blend of teenage hormones topped off with an extra dose of athletic testosterone makes for a hell of a boner-inducing drug.

I ignore the chatter around me and lean forward under the spray, just breathing as the water rushes over me. I give it a few minutes to do its work before giving myself a quick lather and rinse and flipping off the faucet.

I turn to reach for my towel and find myself standing three feet from an equally naked Darryn.

Who's staring right back at me.

Time stretches like taffy around me as I take in every detail—broad shoulders, defined chest, six-pack abs, strong legs, and yeah, the dark hair and soft cock between his thighs.

Time starts moving again with an almost physical jerk, and my gaze snaps back up to meet his. My face heats, but I still can't move until finally he blinks and spins on his heel, breaking the spell. I keep myself from watching him leave, but the damage is done. I've seen Darryn naked before, mostly fleeting glances or from the side or back. Somehow, in the year that we've been teammates and roommates, I'd never managed to get a full-on, full-frontal view of Darryn until now.

Now that I have, the image of his body is seared on my brain. I just want to live in that moment until it fills me—

mind, body, and soul.

Wrapping the towel around my waist, I silently order my dick to behave and march toward my locker, dripping all the way. I'm shivering by the time I get there, the chill having the added benefit of deflating my semi. I'm dried off and dressed in record time, and I hitch my backpack over one shoulder as I make a beeline for the door, dropping my used towel in the oversized laundry hamper on my way.

I step into the gym only to find myself face to face with Rich.

Yep. The universe is *totally* out to get me today.

Rich looks about as pleased to see me as I am to see him. He lifts his chin toward the door. "Darryn in there?"

"Yeah." It's all I can manage. I shift right to walk around him, but his next words stop me in my tracks.

"He's just as good in bed as you think he is."

It takes every ounce of willpower in my body not to turn around and slam my fist into his smarmy face. How *dare* this asshole talk about Darryn like that? He should have some respect for the man who's supposed to be his boyfriend. My fingers curl into a fist, but the thought of Darryn's reaction keeps me from pummeling the guy into a pulp. Rich is Darryn's boyfriend, and Darryn is my friend.

I repeat that mantra—*Darryn's my friend, Darryn's my friend*—under my breath as I ignore the asshole and stalk away. Thankfully, the asshole keeps his trap shut. One more word from him and nothing would've held me back. Never mind that I would've ended up injured, probably suspended from the team, and on the receiving end of Darryn's fury.

I keep myself under control, but the mental image of Rich's bloodied and bruised face brings a grim, dark smile to my face. If I can't mete out the damage I wish I could inflict, at least I can enjoy the idea of it.

Chapter Four

The rest of the week passes in the usual blur of classes, practice, studying, and sleep. Darryn surprises me by staying in our room every night, and except for the cloud of awkward hanging between us, things are pretty okay. Rich doesn't come around the gym again, which helps keep my temper under wraps.

That changes on Thursday. I've just finished my second run-through of my high bar routine and am waiting for one more shot when Rich walks in. He doesn't come far inside, staying near the door and sweeping his gaze over the room. I know the moment he finds Darryn; he freezes, and then he scowls. I glance in the direction he's facing and see Darryn sitting astride the horse with his hands on the pommels. Coach Everson is standing next to him, one hand laying over one of Darryn's, and I can't help rolling my eyes.

Tell me this guy isn't jealous over *that*?

"Clark! You're up!"

Coach Sato's shout brings me back to attention, and I step up to the bar. He gives me a boost up, and I shut out all thoughts of Rich, Darryn, and anything beyond the apparatus as I kip up into a handstand. I let my body swing low and back around the bar, letting go with one hand to make one turn and then re-grasping the bar facing the opposite direction.

My mind rattles off the moves as my body performs them like rote—*stalder, pirouette, back giant, pike, Russian giant*. The Tkatchev goes perfectly, and my double-pike dismount ends in a stuck landing.

A "yeah!" comes from somewhere behind me, and I clap my hands together, chalk dusting the air.

"All right, Clark." I spin to face Coach Sato. "Good job, but don't get cocky. We've still got three months to get your final routine into shape before the Winter Invitational. Plenty of difficulty yet to go."

I give a nod, but it doesn't slow my heart as it thumps in my chest. I know it's not a final routine—not with months still to go until the competition that launches the official season—but that felt *good*. As good as I ever have on high bar, and close to how I usually feel on the floor. I wish I could bottle that and carry it around with me, like liquid luck.

A whistle shrills. "Okay, that's it!" Coach Everson's voice booms across the floor. "Good workout today. Take it easy this weekend, don't get hurt. Be ready to hit it hard again on Monday." He grins for a hot second. "Now get outta here."

His obvious satisfaction with our progress buoys the team as a group as we head for the locker room. I'm a couple of feet behind Darryn, lagging behind the crowd, and I'm about to take a few long steps to draw even with him when Rich appears out of nowhere and grabs Darryn's hand, pulling him to a stop.

"Hey. Let's get out of here," he says, a pleading note in his voice that I haven't heard before. "I don't want to be late for tonight."

Darryn gives him a small smile. "I need to shower and

change first."

"Takes too long, and I've got a surprise waiting." Rich's gaze flicks to where I've stopped on the other side of Darryn, and he scowls. "Besides, you never know what kind of perv might be getting himself an eyeful in the showers."

A shock runs through me. No way Darryn told Rich about our unplanned starefest in the showers. No *way*.

Darryn doesn't react to Rich's provocation, just pulls his hands free. "You know it's not like that. I'll be out in a few minutes. Promise."

For a second, I think Rich is going to object, but he gives me another look and then glances toward where Coach Sato and Coach Everson are going over notes together in the middle of the gym. He takes a step back. "All right. I'll be waiting."

Darryn nods and walks away. I follow, after throwing a double handful of visual daggers in Rich's direction.

I find Darryn at his locker, pulling his clothes out of his duffel. "What crawled up his ass and died?"

Darryn snorts. "He made reservations for dinner, Grant. If I don't hurry, we'll be late."

He pulls off his snug tank and swipes at his skin with his towel. I hardly even notice his body, still focused on Rich's behavior.

"You've got time to shower, don't you?" I wave a hand at the towel. "I mean, two minutes will get the sweat off so you aren't sticky."

"It's fine." He finishes drying his face and torso, and drops the towel on the bench before reaching into his locker for a bottle of body spray. "I'll get a shower later. Don't make it into some big deal."

It sure seems like a big deal, but I'm not going to get anywhere by arguing with him. I force myself to relax and reach for my own towel. "Okay then," I tell him, doing my best to make my voice sound teasing. "But don't come whining to me later when you feel itchy and gross."

I turn toward the showers, unwilling to stand there watching Darryn strip down in front of me before heading off for a date with his boyfriend. It's not like I need another look anyway. That view's already permanently imprinted on my brain.

· · ·

Monday afternoon, we're only a few minutes into practice when Rich shows up *again*. He doesn't approach Darryn this time, just heads over to the bleachers and takes a seat right up front. Darryn gives him a long look and then flicks his gaze over to me for just a second before he turns back to the pommel horse. I'm up next on floor, but I spare a second to throw a withering glare in Rich's direction before I get started.

I feel like I'm being watched the whole time. Not like Coach or the other guys watching. Like a burn. Like if looks could kill, I'd be laid out flat.

When I finally give up on playing dumb and look in Rich's direction, he's staring at me as if he expects me to spontaneously combust on the spot.

Asshole.

When practice finally ends, what feels like several weeks later, I end up behind Darryn on the way to the locker room. Rich heads in Darryn's direction again, but before he gets there, Darryn's made it into the locker room.

Rich turns on me instead.

"Can't stand it, can you?" He keeps his voice low enough not to attract the attention of the coaches still standing across the gym floor. "Knowing the guy you've got the hots for has a real man in his bed. Not some little wannabe wimp."

Do not let him get to you. I bare my teeth at him in a mockery of a smile. "No real man would feel the need to goad his boyfriend's roommate over some imagined rivalry. Darryn can think for himself."

I turn toward the locker room doors, but I can't help hearing Rich's parting shot. "He doesn't need to. I can do the thinking for both of us."

The words sink in after I'm inside, and I fight off the urge to go back and confront him about it. My concern is with Darryn, not with whatever mind game Rich thinks he's playing.

At least this time Darryn's not rushing out to meet Rich. He's headed toward the showers when I get to my locker, and I decide to wait until he's done to take my turn. No sense in tempting hormonal fate.

I strip out of my practice uniform slowly and wrap a towel around my waist before taking a seat on the bench. I zone out, letting the noises of my teammates trading barbs and getting changed wash over me, the sound soothing after so many years.

I lose track of time until a towel drops over my head.

"Napping on the job, Clark?"

"I'm on break!" The retort is out before I even realize who I'm talking to. "Oh." I sit up straighter. "Hey, Coach."

Coach Everson smirks down at me. "When you're back in street clothes, come by my office. Nothing bad," he adds, this time with a quick grin. "Just a couple of questions for you."

I nod. "Sure thing, Coach."

He turns on his heel, and as he walks away, I finally drag myself to my feet and head toward the showers. If Darryn's still in there, I'll have to live with it.

Just as I reach the doorway, though, Darryn passes me on his way out. He flashes me a fleeting smile, and I do my best to return it just as fleetingly and without staring at his bare chest.

Dammit. This is driving me crazy, and not only because I'm attracted to him. I miss the easy friendship we had before this whole mess got dropped in between us.

I shower on autopilot, and in minutes I'm back at my locker getting dressed. Darryn's long gone by then, and I force my mind away from thinking about who he's with and what he's doing. I finish dressing, shove my dirty gear into my gym bag, and slam my locker shut before heading toward Coach's office.

The school's athletic facilities are new, like everything in a college that's only a few years old, but that doesn't mean they're spacious. Coach Everson's office has room for his desk, a couple of guest chairs, and TV setup for watching tapes. Coach Sato's office is a glorified coat closet, and even that description's generous.

I knock on the doorframe, and Coach doesn't look up from the paper in his hand as he waves me toward one of the chairs. I push the door shut behind me just in case. Even if it's not anything bad, it might not be anything I want to be overheard.

"I have a proposal for you. Bob Wheeler and I were talking a few days ago about starting a student coaching program."

The athletic director is in on this? I sit up straighter, suddenly feeling as if I'm interviewing for a job.

"You did a good job with Kenny the other day," Coach continues, "and I know you talked about wanting to coach. Do you think you might be interested in something like that?"

I nod. "I would, sir. What did you have in mind?"

Coach leans back in his chair and crosses his arms. "We're still working out specifics. And it would likely be for upperclassmen only, so you'd have to be at least a junior to qualify. But Coach Sato and I both did some student coaching work in undergrad, and we think it's a good program."

"I think it would be great," I reply. "Good experience for the students, on both sides, and great for the program as a whole." I'm mostly talking out of my ass, but it sounds good, so I press on. "I'd definitely be interested in applying for next year."

"I'm glad to hear that." Coach grins. "My job is to feel out enthusiasm among our students. It probably would be opened to the other sports programs, too. I can't guarantee we'd have a spot for you if we do a pilot program next year."

"I understand." At least we don't have a football program to fend off. Baseball, softball, tennis, swimming, diving, and gymnastics. Small school, small athletic department.

"Thanks, Clark." Coach leans forward. "I'd appreciate it if you kept this between us for now." He reaches for a folder on his desk. "Now get out of here."

"Sure thing, Coach."

I'm up and out the door before I realize it, excitement buzzing in my stomach and making me bounce on my toes like I'm on the floor exercise mat. When I leave the locker room, the only people in sight are the custodial crew, working on cleaning up after a bunch of messy college students. One of the guys gives me a smile and a "You have a good day, now," and I smile back as I hit the outside door.

I head toward my dorm, steps still light, the smile refusing to leave my face—at least, until I think of Darryn.

My steps slow. I have no idea if Darryn will be in the room when I get back, though I'd lay odds that he's off with Rich somewhere. That's probably a good thing, because it'll give me time to come down from my giddiness. Then I'll be less likely to blurt out what Coach asked me to keep to myself.

It'll also give me way too much time to think too much about what, exactly, Darryn and Rich are doing right now.

Damn, my life is a freaking rollercoaster. I just hope it doesn't decide to jump the tracks.

• • •

When Darryn gets back to the room that night, he's practically glowing, and it makes me want to throw things. Preferably at Rich's head.

"Hey." I keep my voice neutral. Ish.

"Hey." Darryn doesn't seem to notice anything. He tosses his gym bag on his bed and opens the second drawer of his dresser, digging out a loose pair of shorts. "You up for a study session tonight? I stayed with Rich too long and need to get caught up on some reading."

"Sure." I was only watching videos on my phone anyway. "Why did...I mean, what had you hung up with Rich?"

I don't choke on the name, but it's a close thing. Darryn smiles wider. "I'm happy that he came to watch practice today. It's the first time he's shown a real interest in my gymnastics."

My face screws up at that. "Really?"

"Yeah." Darryn's still smiling as he strips off his jeans and pulls on the shorts. "He's usually grumbling about me going to practice because he wants to be with me."

"That's kinda...um, weird?" I can't quite articulate what I mean. The way Darryn stiffens and his smile slips, though, I better figure it out fast. "I mean, it's a couple of hours a day. Is he afraid to let you out of his sight?"

And that was the totally wrong thing to say. Darryn's face goes dark. "He wants to be with me," he snaps. "There's nothing wrong with that. Jealousy isn't a good look for you."

I have to fight hard against the automatic urge to lash out in return. Yeah, I'm jealous, but that's not why this is bothering me. I still can't figure out how to say why it's bothering me, though, and it's pretty clear Darryn's not going to listen anyway.

"That came out wrong," I say instead. "I'm sorry. I'm glad you're glad, okay?"

It's clearly not okay, but Darryn's apparently willing to make the same effort I am, not to have a screaming match over it. He visibly relaxes. "Okay." He gives me a look somewhere between placating and pleading. "I know this isn't easy, okay? I don't expect you to be happy about it."

I bark out a laugh. "I'm pretty sure happy is the furthest from how I feel about it."

His gaze drops. "I can imagine."

And it hits me then that he *can* imagine. What if this whole thing were reversed? He'd been crushing on me almost as long as I'd been crushing on him. What if I'd been the one to start dating someone else and Darryn had been the one left behind?

I get a twinge of vindictive glee at the thought—*schadenfreudelicious!*—but I quash that fast. I'm not *that* much of an asshole.

"Yeah." My voice is soft. "I guess I just wish things were different."

Darryn nods. "I get that. But here we are." He blows out a breath and grabs a book off his desk. "And on that note, I really have to get this reading done tonight. Dr. Chopra never tells us outright when he's planning a quiz, but he loves to drop big hints. 'Might want to get your reading done tonight instead of putting it off until the weekend again,' stuff like that."

"Helpful." I reach for my own backpack where it sits next to my bed. "Studying, huh? I remember that. Something freshmen do, right?"

Darryn barks out a laugh. "I'm pretty sure we were the only freshmen who ever put studying ahead of partying. Or at least the only ones in our class."

"Kept us on the team," I point out in our defense as I crack open my anthropology book. "Some guys weren't as lucky." We had only one teammate suspended for low grades, but I know several more got kicked off other teams. U of A's athletic programs are small enough that we all pretty much know each other, and gossip travels fast.

"All right. Buddy bet." Darryn names the game that kept us on track most of the previous year. "An hour studying. No talking." Yeah, okay, keeping my mouth shut is a struggle. "If you make it, I'll get snacks. If you don't, you're on the hook. Deal?"

"Deal."

I nearly always lose these bets. It's next to impossible for me to keep my mouth shut for that long. I do have one special dispensation—I can repeat a sentence aloud to help me absorb it. I do that unconsciously so often that it'd be unfair to count that against me.

Of course, the snacks I pick out are usually more fun than Darryn's. He's not a diet hard-ass by any means, but he'll get fruit juice and pretzels instead of soda and chocolate. Unless it's dark chocolate, of course. He does keep a stash of his favorite Japanese snacks around, though—melon pan, mochi, Pocky, even dried seaweed—and sometimes he'll share.

Okay, well. I'm not such a fan of the seaweed, I'll admit.

We're both quiet for the first little while. Sounds from outside our room filter in—doors closing down the hall, water running, people shouting and laughing outside. Darryn's highlighter squeaks as he marks a passage, and then the paper flips as he turns the page.

I'm only half absorbing what I'm reading. Too much of my attention is focused on the man sitting across the room from me.

This has been the problem with the two of us studying together almost since we first met. I'd been caught off guard by the way my stomach swooped when Coach Everson brought him over to introduce him and Darryn smiled, friendly but a little unsure. Being out to myself was a brand-new thing then, and my sister was the only other one who knew. I wonder now if Darryn had felt the same thing. Maybe if I'd been up front with him from the start…

It takes an effort to pull my thoughts out of that valley and back to the page in front of me. Anthropology ought to be more interesting than this, but the text is dry and the professor almost as bad. If it wasn't "strongly suggested" for my major, I'd have gone for something else.

Darryn's in psychology, which doesn't sound much better, though he's had good things to say about his professor. And here I am thinking about him instead of doing my reading again. Argh. I give up and read the next lines out loud.

"An example of an old ritual that is encoded in myth and religious symbolism can be found in the catacombs of Sicily where over 2,000 dead bodies are kept. Most of these bodies have been embalmed or mummified and dressed in the attire that suited their profession, many of them being nobles, professionals, and merchants."

Darryn's head pops up. "Okay, that's gross," he says, and then his eyes widen as he realizes what he's done. "Oh shit!"

I'm laughing already. "You lose! And none of that uber-healthy stuff this time, either. I want at least a Snickers out of you."

Darryn grumbles under his breath, but there's a hint of a smile on his face as he turns back to his text. I know I can't stop smiling, and for a moment, it feels like it did before. I wish I could hold onto that feeling, but just the act of thinking about it bursts the bubble.

It's not the same. It never will be. I've got to accept it. What are the stages of grief? I guess Darryn's textbook would cover that. Denial, anger, depression…whatever. Acceptance comes eventually. Right now, I keep bouncing between anger and depression. It's giving me whiplash, and it's getting old fast.

Dammit. I shake my head and force myself back to my reading. I'm never going to learn anything about religion and ritual at the rate I'm going.

I wish there were a textbook to spell out how to navigate through the newly mined field of my relationship with Darryn.

Chapter Five

All right, nail this last fucking tumbling pass, you asshole.

Even on a good day, my internal monologue during a routine sometimes sounds like Deadpool and Samuel L. Jackson as the Spartan cheerleaders—equal parts rah-rah-sis-boom-bah and "do you even *do* gymnastics, fucker?"

Today? Today is not the best day.

Rich is here again. Sitting in that same spot in the bleachers, this time ignoring me and watching Darryn like a hawk. Twice I've caught him baring his teeth when someone else touched Darryn, even though one was a high-five and the other was Coach Sato lifting him up to grasp the rings.

This guy is a real piece of work.

I do my best to channel my anger and frustration into my routine. I nail the tumbling pass, and when I jog off the edge of the mat to let Kenny take his turn, I feel marginally better.

Then I glance over at Darryn and catch him frowning toward Rich, and all that emotion wells back up like it never went anywhere at all.

I make it through the rest of practice without exploding,

which feels like a feat of valor, and I stand under a hot shower longer than I usually would, ignoring all my teammates, including—especially—Darryn. I trudge back to my locker and dress, and when I turn to leave, I'm surprised to see Darryn waiting for me.

"Hey," he says with the tiniest of smiles. "You gonna be studying tonight? I could use another buddy bet."

I muster up a smile about the same quality as his. "Sure. Always more reading."

"Great. I'm having dinner… I mean, I'll be back after dinner. Maybe around eight?"

I shove away the knot in my stomach at the knowledge of who he's having dinner with—you'd think I'd be used to it by now—and give a nod. "I'll be there."

Darryn turns toward the door and pulls it open before waving me through. "I won't lose this time, so better get your wallet ready."

"We'll see about that." I taunt as we walk out into the gym together.

Our banter gets cut short because seconds later, Rich is there. He bares his teeth in a semblance of a smile, but his eyes tell me an entirely different story.

"Come on, babe," he slimes out as he wraps his fingers around Darryn's upper arm. "Let's get out of here. I missed you so much."

I don't even have a chance to respond before Rich is dragging Darryn away. Darryn says something to Rich in a low voice, and Rich responds by slowing down and sliding his hand down to take Darryn's hand instead of holding onto his arm, but they're still out the door within another few seconds.

I shake my head, as if I can shake off the entire encounter and maybe Rich's whole existence. Blowing out a breath, I hike my bag higher on my shoulder and head out to find some dinner.

• • •

As promised, Darryn comes through the door of our room at eight p.m. sharp. He flashes me that same tiny little smile and drops his bag on his bed, going through the usual ritual of toeing off his sneakers and trading his jeans for loose shorts. He grabs a book and a highlighter off his desk and drops onto his bed.

"Sorry about Rich," he says after a moment. "He knows we're close, and he gets jealous sometimes. I tell him we're just friends, but, well." He shrugs.

He's a controlling bastard? I bite my lips to hold back the words and return his shrug. "It's okay. I get it."

It's a lie, but it's the best I can come up with.

Darryn settles against the wall and opens his book. He picks up his phone. "Buddy bet?"

I turn back to my own book. "Buddy bet."

"All right." His phone beeps. "Annnnd, go!"

Right off the bat, we fall into the same rhythm as always, the scratch of a pen and the soft shushing noise of a highlighter joining the soft music coming from my phone as we work. I'm not completely focused, I'll admit. A small voice in the back of my mind reminds me that Darryn not only came back to study with me—he cut short his time with Rich to do it. There might be a little bit of mental dancing going on.

But homework's still a thing. I try to push all that aside and concentrate. I make it through the entire hour, the stopwatch sounding seconds before I push my book aside. "Ugh. There's only so much anthropology my brain can absorb at a time."

Darryn laughs. "Definitely time for a break," he agrees.

As if scripted, his phone chimes, and he reaches over to check his text. His face rolls through about four different expressions as he reads—a happy smile, followed by a furrowed brow and a frown before he shakes his head and types out a short reply. He puts the phone down and reaches for his water bottle to take a long pull, then balances it on his book and fiddles with the mouthpiece.

I watch him fidget, wondering what he has on his mind—because it's pretty clear he's working his way up to saying something.

"Rich wants me to move in with him."

Wait, *what*?

"I told him it's too soon," he adds quickly, probably to head off anything I might say. "We haven't been dating that long. And I'm not supposed to move off campus until junior year anyway. He hasn't quite let it go yet."

He might as well have slapped me across the face. "How long would be long enough?" I choke out.

Darryn slumps against the wall. "I don't know," he admits, his voice shaky. "Just...not this soon."

Anger wells up in my chest. "Then he should leave you alone about it." I slam my book shut. "No means no."

Darryn shoots me a glare. "It's not like that. He wants to spend more time with me, you know? It's what boyfriends do."

The idea of Darryn moving in with Rich leaves me sick to my stomach, and not only because I still have a thing for him. I already feel like I'm losing my best friend. I don't want to lose my roommate, too.

I take a steadying breath and lift a placating hand. "I didn't mean anything by it." A lie, but I hope it's a convincing one. "But you know what he wants, and you said no. You can tell him if you're ever ready for something like that. He shouldn't keep pressuring you about it."

His expression softens. "It's okay. I mean, I'd have to agree to it. Not like he can kidnap me and make me go."

Some tension drains out of me at that, and I chuckle.

"Yeah, I think people would notice."

"Anyway." Darryn sets his water bottle down and pushes his books aside. "I know that was only, like, an hour, but I think my brain is shot for tonight. I'm gonna wash up and brush my teeth, get to bed a little early."

"Sounds like a plan." I watch him climb to his feet and grab his shower caddy to head across the hall. After he's gone, I sit there another couple of seconds, feeling like I'm missing something, before I finally shove my own books aside to go take another shower.

Maybe the water will knock loose whatever I'm not quite grasping.

• • •

I still haven't figured it out by lunch the next day. I got to the dining hall late, and they don't have much of anything that looks appetizing, at least for the mood I'm in. So I have a half-assed salad and bottle of apple juice. I'm digging through wilted romaine for an elusive bacon bit when Annie plops down in a seat across the table from me. She's followed by Mo—Michelle—who'd been Annie's roommate freshman year, before Annie saved up enough from her side hustle to pay the extra fees for a single room.

Annie immediately narrows her eyes at me. "You look like the subject of a bad country song."

I bark out something approximating a laugh. "Isn't that redundant?"

Annie snorts and shakes her own bottle of juice. "Touché." She glances around. "Where's the roomie?"

I shrug, still chasing bacon. "Probably with his boyfriend again."

Annie makes a noise that falls somewhere between mocking and sympathetic. "Still dealing with the other dude?"

"He's an asshole." I stab a grape tomato with more force than necessary. "He's just always there, you know? He's even showing up to practices now. And he cannot *stand* when anyone touches Darryn, even when it's one of the coaches correcting his positioning. And I hardly see him anymore. Darryn, I mean. He comes to our room to sleep most nights… during the week, at least. But he's always with Rich."

I growl out the name and stab another tomato, hitting it at the right angle with my fork that it goes flying off the table and rolls across the floor. I blow out a breath and look up in time to see Annie and Mo exchange a long look. Before I can ask what that's about, Annie tips her chin at Mo, and Mo nods before turning toward me.

"Is Darryn doing things differently?" she asks. "I mean, other than going out with Rich a lot. Has he stopped doing anything he normally does? Stopped talking to anyone?"

I frown. "Not… I mean, he's not around much, but he's with Rich." Now she has me thinking. "And he doesn't go to the library or the gym like we used to." I shrug it off. "But we did a lot of that stuff together, so it'd probably be kind of awkward."

"Is he still doing that stuff, just without you, though?" Annie's gaze is sharp. "You said Rich started coming to practice all of a sudden. Is he keeping tabs on Darryn? Keeping him away from you?"

I shake my head, though my gut clenches. "You guys are overreacting. They're dating. Of course they spend a lot of time together. That's what people who are dating do."

I pull up short as I realize I'm parroting Darryn's words. *Why the hell am I making excuses for Rich?*

Mo doesn't let it slide. "They don't normally cut you off from other people, and they don't monitor what you do." Mo folds her arms on the tabletop and leans forward. "Trust us.

Women hear a lot about this stuff. How to tell if a guy's being controlling. If he's trying to isolate you. Warning signs."

Now she's lost me. "Warning signs?"

"Abuse, asshat." Annie gives me a look like I've been dropped on my head repeatedly. "Classic progression. Cut the victim off from any kind of support so when the really bad stuff kicks in, he's got no one to go to."

Gobsmacked is the only way I can describe how I feel. "You seriously think—"

I cut off my own train of thought as the progression of the past few weeks runs through my mind. They might have heard more than I did, but Annie and Mo weren't the only ones who got the freshman year orientation warnings about how to spot bad situations. Darryn's practically disappeared from everything except class and practice. Rich started out showing up at the end of practice and waiting until Darryn was ready to go, but then he started getting there earlier and rushing Darryn out the second we're done. Darryn's been MIA at dinner most nights, when we used to eat nearly every meal together, and he comes back to the room late—when he comes back at all.

My stomach twists, and my fork slips out of my fingers. "That's... I mean, I haven't seen anything that makes me think he'd *hit* Darryn."

"Abuse isn't just about hitting." Mo catches my gaze and holds it, and something in her eyes tells me this isn't only speculation on her part. "It's about control. Emotional and verbal abuse is as bad as physical, and sometimes it's even harder to get over."

I can only nod in response.

"So," Annie puts in. "Keep an eye on things. Watch how they interact. If Darryn starts acting weird about being around Rich, ask him about it."

"Be careful about it," Mo adds. "His first instinct is

going to be to protect the boyfriend. More than anything, he's going to need you to be his friend. Don't give the asshole more reasons to paint you as the enemy."

My head is swimming. "I'll pay attention," I promise. I can't be sure, of course, but everything they're telling me feels right. I should've realized sooner what was behind that weird feeling about Rich I couldn't figure out. Maybe it wasn't just jealousy after all.

I muster up a small smile. "If I need help dealing with it, I know where to go, right, ladies?"

"Payment due up front." Annie sticks her tongue out at me, and I toss a balled-up napkin at her in response.

Mo sighs. "Gotta love twin rivalry," she mutters as she reaches for her glass.

Well, I don't want her to feel left out. I ball up another napkin and toss it her way. She bats it off with an ease that makes me blink before I remember her sport.

Annie laughs at me. "Maybe you should stick to the gym and leave the balls to the experts."

I can't help myself. I push back far enough to glance down at my crotch and then back up at her. "I'm pretty sure I'm an expert at balls, thanks."

"I'm pretty sure you don't want me slamming a racket into those." Mo's grin is entirely too much like Annie's, and two women versus one sensitive set of gonads is more than I want to take on. I press my legs tightly together and concede defeat.

"So, Mo," I say, forking up some corn, "How are things on the courts these days?"

They're still laughing at me, but they must be feeling benevolent, because they accept the change of subject.

If only I could stop worrying about Darryn that easily.

• • •

The next afternoon, my phone buzzes with a text as I'm walking to practice. It's Annie, a rarity. For someone so absorbed in computers and technology, she sure doesn't use any of it as much as most college students do.

Mo was looking for you. Wondered if you wanted to go to Pride this weekend with her.

I stare down at the phone, wondering how that subject came up—is Mo gay, too?—but before I can respond, a second text follows the first: *And no, I didn't out you. She figured it out on her own. She said, and I quote, "That boy needs someone to show him the rainbow ropes."*

My first instinct is to say *oh hell no*. I've never been to Atlanta Pride, or any gay-pride-related event at all. All I know is what I've read online, and I've never really thought about going.

I make myself consider it now. Sexuality aside, Mo would certainly be a safe tour guide for a Big Gay Adventure. And maybe it'll get me out of my head and give me something to focus on other than what's going on with Darryn.

Sure, I send back. *Give her my number and we'll plan. But you're going with us.*

What? No way.

I grin as I reply. *Yes way. Clear your schedule!*

I shove my phone back in my pocket, ignoring the buzz as Annie tries to argue, and open the door to the gym. The familiar scents of sweat, plastic, and chalk smell like coming home. I deliberately don't look toward the stands, keeping my gaze focused on the locker room door until I'm through it and safely inside.

I change into my practice gear on autopilot and then sit on the bench, waiting for Darryn to show up. He still isn't there by the time the clock on the wall hits ten till three, though, and I start to worry. He's never been this late to practice, and last night he didn't come home. Add that to my conversation with Annie and Mo, and I can't help worrying. But I also can't stay in the locker room any longer unless I want to deal with unhappy coaches.

I reach the door out to the gym floor as Darryn darts inside. "Sorry, running late!" he calls as he hurries toward our lockers. I want to follow him, make sure he's okay, but at a quick glance he seems fine, just rushed. I leave him to change and head on out into the gym, resolving to talk to him after practice.

I don't look over where he usually sits, but I can feel Rich's gaze on me as I cross to the mats and go into my usual warm-up routine. I don't look back. If he wants to glower his way through our practices, well, whatever. It's his wasted time, not mine.

Darryn jogs out to join the team a few minutes later, and I keep half an eye on him while he warms up. He still seems to be okay, no signs of wariness or fear, and he doesn't look toward Rich. The knot in my stomach loosens. Maybe things are fine. Maybe I'm seeing things that aren't there. Maybe I want Darryn too much, and it's coloring the way I look at Rich.

Or maybe everything Annie and Mo said is right, and I need to keep my guard up in case the whole thing blows up in our faces.

Chapter Six

"Here."

I blink down at the giant cup under my nose as my brain registers the smell of the coffee inside. "Oh my God, you're my favorite person." I practically moan the words as I take the cup out of Mo's hand.

She laughs and bumps her hip against mine—or several inches above my hip, actually, considering our height difference. "Gotta get you awake before we get to the festival."

Annie's on Mo's other side, both hands wrapped around her own cup of liquid gold. Mo wraps her free arm around Annie's shoulder and turns toward the MARTA station across the street from the coffee shop that she'd made our first stop.

"C'mon," she cajoles us. "Just a little bit farther and you can sit down to finish your coffee."

We're on the train in another fifteen minutes, and by the time we reach Midtown, the car is full to bursting. Annie and I are both more alert after the caffeine infusion, though she sticks close to Mo's side as we navigate the crowds. Finding the way to the exit is no problem at all, though.

"Follow the rainbows," Mo mutters.

I snicker. "They're after me Lucky Charms!"

That earns me a backhand to the biceps, and even as a joke, it stings. Mo packs a wallop. "Hey, not a tennis ball over here," I protest, rubbing the sore spot.

"Gotta keep in practice." Mo grins, grabs Annie by the hand, and then takes off down the sidewalk, her long legs eating up the concrete. Annie's left almost running to match Mo's pace, and I rush to catch up, dodging around clumps of colorfully dressed people, following Mo's head of natural curls. She usually has it corralled into a ponytail, which I imagine would be a hell of a lot easier to deal with on the courts. Today she's left it free. The style suits her, and I see more than one head turn as she passes.

I can't blame them. She's not my type, of course, but her height and her graceful, athletic movements make her a standout.

My own hair blows into my face as I catch up with her, and I shove it back out of the way. "I'm thinking man bun, yeah?" I follow up the words by pulling my hair back with both hands and stifle a laugh as Annie's eyes nearly roll right out of her head.

"You couldn't have pulled that off even when everyone was doing it."

Mo squints, her gaze zeroing in on my jawline. "And you'd need more than that little bit of peach fuzz to get the whole lumbersexual thing going anyway."

I sigh and let my hair drop. "Yeah, never could get anything resembling a decent beard going."

"S'okay." Mo winks at me. "The young-and-freckly look works for you. Plus, all that gym work means you've got muscles for days. You gotta *werk* it, babe."

She puts a swish and swing into her next few steps before

she bursts out laughing, and I have to join in. All the weight of everything that's been holding me back for the past few weeks flies away like it was never there, and I resolve to forget the crap and enjoy the day.

Annie, meanwhile, looks at us both like we're off our rockers. "Is this what you two are going to be like all day?"

"Probably," Mo shoots back.

Just then, shouting comes from off to our left, and Mo grabs both of us by the hand and pulls us in the other direction. "Yeah, no. Not dealing with the uber fundies today."

As she drags us away, I get a glimpse of a clump of people on the sidewalk holding garish signs and yelling. I can read only a few words, but they're more than enough for me to be happy to avoid them.

"Is it always like that?"

Mo squeezes my hand before letting both of us go. "Yep. It'll be worse for the parade tomorrow. They always have a bunch of different groups all along the route. Pride always brings out the religious nuts."

I guess that's no surprise. I just hadn't experienced it firsthand before. Of course, I haven't experienced Pride firsthand, either. I'm betting the overall day will end up being a hell of a lot more positive.

The view as we walk into the park confirms my thought. The sheer number of rainbows would be enough, but there are couples holding hands everywhere and bright colors in all directions, flags and banners and clothes and hair. Tattoos and piercings adorn more bodies than not, and nearly every face bears a wide smile.

It's like we've stepped into an alternate reality where no one hides and everyone can happily be exactly who they are on the inside.

It's hard to describe how incredibly freeing it is.

Suddenly I wish we'd brought Darryn along today. I know

I needed some time away from everything, and the festival going on around me certainly fits that bill. But as much as I don't know how he'd feel about being surrounded by so many bold expressions of queer life, I want to share this feeling with him. I want him to know that there's a bright, big world out here, and it's waiting for us to jump right in.

I pause long enough to take a picture of the colorful crowd and shoot it off to Darryn with a simple message: *Wish you were here!*

I hurry to catch up with Mo and Annie, who stopped at the nearest booth to wait for me. They don't ask who I was texting—their knowing smiles tell me they already know.

"Okay." I wave an arm. "You ready to show us the gayer side of life?"

Mo laughs and leads the way. The farther we wander into the park, the larger and more diverse the crowd around us grows. Mo keeps moving, only slowing down a few times to glance into a few of the vendor booths we pass. Annie keeps pace with Mo, and I follow a few steps behind, trying not to gawk too much at the many shirtless men we pass. Yeah, sue me. I like guys, and even though my heart belongs to one guy in particular right now, I'm going to look when I'm surrounded by so many hot ones. I try not to stare, but...

"See anything you like?"

Whoops. Guess I'm not as discreet as I thought. Mo had paused to grab something from a vendor's table, and my eyes had landed on the body of a big, beefy, hairy guy wearing low-slung jeans and a leather harness. My face burns at his smirking scrutiny, but I give him a hesitant smile.

"Sorry, he's a newbie." Mo's back, and she bumps her shoulder against mine as she shoots Big and Beefy a grin. She turns her head toward me and bursts into laughter. "Wow, your face almost matches your hair!"

Big and Beefy chuckles, and Mo grabs my hand again.

"C'mon, Studly. You need more than ten minutes at Pride before you run off for a hookup."

She turns her smile back toward Big and Beefy as she leads me away to where Annie stands a couple of feet away, snickering behind her hand. I give the guy a shrug as I follow. She's right. Even if I did decide to try to pick someone up today—and even if big, beefy, and leather-wearing were my type—I'm here for the full experience. Festival first, then other kinds of fun.

The smell of grilling meat and hot grease hits me as we round the next corner, making my stomach growl. Okay, maybe food before anything else.

A line of food vendors stretches out in front of us, each one with big, bigger, and biggest banners proclaiming their wares. The signs promised everything from burgers and fries to various meats on a stick to vegan and vegetarian fare to deep-fried everything.

"Foooood." I hold my arms out in front of me and shamble, zombie-like, toward the buffet. "Must. Have. Fooooood."

Mo snorts. "Take your pick, Studly."

After careful consideration for all of a minute or two, I end up going for an overstuffed gyro with a side of curly fries and a big cup of fresh-squeezed lemonade. Balancing everything carefully, I cross to where some small groupings of tables and chairs are set up in a grassy area and snag a place for us. Mo and Annie follow me a few minutes later, each carrying a rice bowl, heavy on the veggies, and their own lemonades.

We settle down to eat, but a few bites in, Mo swallows and points off to one side. "We can hit up the artsy-fartsy section after this if you want. A lot of the booths are, like, corporations and stuff like that, but there's a whole section that'll have some cool artwork to check out. Probably out of our price range, but browsing is free."

I shrug and pick up a fry. "Whatever you want is fine with me. You're the tour guide."

Mo laughs and forks up more food. "Grant and Annie Clark, Welcome to Your Gay Life!"

"Insert rainbow here." Annie sketches out an arc in the air with one hand, and Mo punctuates it with a bit of jazz hands.

We grin at each other before digging back into our food.

. . .

Seven hours later, I'm about ready to leave The Gay Life behind.

"I'm going to die."

Mo laughs and throws an arm around my shoulders. "Wimp. Aren't you supposed to be an athlete?"

I whimper as I pick up my feet one at a time, trying to shake off the aches. Annie's already given up and slumped against the wall where we stand on the platform at the MARTA station, surrounded by other worn-out festivalgoers. "Walking one-point-two million miles all over Midtown uses an entirely different set of muscles than tumbling passes," I point out. "And you spend a lot more time on your feet than I do."

Annie groans. "Stop talking about feet. I'm trying to ignore that mine exist."

The next train pulls in before Mo can respond, and seconds later, we're inside and I'm letting out a sigh of relief as I slide into an empty seat next to Annie. Mo plops down across the aisle from us. "Better?"

"Much." I stretch out my legs and rotate my ankles to try to work out the kinks. "Note to self: Pride takes advance training. Plan ahead next year."

"Amen." Annie's got her head tipped against the window and her eyes closed as the train pulls out of the station, heading north toward campus. I resist the urge to lower my head onto her shoulder. I glance back at Mo instead. "The parade's tomorrow?"

"Yeah. You wanna go back for that?"

I bark out a laugh. "I think my feet would go on strike. I was wondering if it'll be on TV or something."

"Don't know." Mo digs into her pocket for her phone. "But I can find out."

I turn my head to watch the city fly by as we speed north. Pride turned out to be everything and nothing like what I expected. Sure, there were plenty of rowdy and even tawdry scenes, but mostly it was like any other kind of festival, full of happy groups of people eating unhealthy food, buying overpriced goods, and enjoying the clear fall day. I'd been sure I'd stick out like I'd just stepped out of a closet—because I had—but I simply felt like one of the crowd.

Having Mo and Annie there helped, of course. Mo pushed us both to spread our wings, and I lost some of my own reticence as I watched Annie's curiosity overcome her innate introversion when she found things that piqued her interest.

I nudge her with my elbow. "Did you have fun?" I ask in a low voice.

She doesn't open her eyes, but a small smile crosses her face. "Yeah. Thanks for making me go, dorkface."

The train heads into a tunnel just as Mo nudges my foot with hers. "Parade's online only. Dammit." She sighs and gives me a frustrated look. "Lost my connection. I can send you the link once I have service again."

"I'm sure I can find it. Google is a thing." I have to spend tomorrow catching up on homework, so if I miss it, there's always next year.

Mo leans forward to rest her forearms on her thighs, arching her back into a slow stretch. "What's the verdict? Are you all in for the queer life?"

I laugh. "Kind of late to hide now." I shrug. "It was fun. It felt..." I'm not sure how to explain that sense of belonging. "It felt... normal, I guess. Like it was no big deal."

Mo pins me with a look. "It *is* normal," she tells me. "I mean, it should be. Yeah, we're gay, but that's one of the ways each of us is unique. Everyone's different, but we're all normal." She grins. "For whatever 'normal' means, anyway."

I give her a genuine smile. "You're good people, Mo."

She smiles back. "Back atcha, hon."

• • •

The next afternoon, I've got the parade set up on my laptop, my attention divided between the flash and sound of the show and the next chapter of the bio textbook on my lap, when the door opens and Darryn walks in.

My instinct is to shut off the parade. To hide. But Darryn already knows the truth, and I remind myself of how I felt yesterday—open and free—and how I wanted to share that with him.

"Hey."

Darryn drops his backpack on his bed. "Hey. Did you have fun with Mo and Annie yesterday?"

"I did." I glance over as he flops onto his bed. He stretches out across the mattress, one arm over his eyes, and toes off his sneakers, letting them tumble onto the floor. His T-shirt rides up as he moves, baring a tantalizing slice of his toned abs, and my stomach clenches.

I push those feelings aside yet again. *Friends, friends, friends*, I remind myself.

"We had a good day," I tell him. "I've got the parade on

now, if you want to watch some of it."

Darryn paused in mid-stretch to look at me for a long moment but then nods. "Sure. How do I...?"

"Bring your chair over," I tell him, rolling mine to the side to make room. "I could probably get this up on the TV..."

"Nah, this is fine." He gets up and pushes his desk chair over to my side, but as soon as he settles in, I'm distracted. I can feel the heat of his thigh a bare inch from mine, smell his woodsy shampoo. I don't know if I can handle him this close to me.

I suck in a breath and let it out slowly as I stare at my laptop screen, trying to keep my composure. The images aren't helping much—a float full of young guys wearing nothing but their underwear, dancing to the pulsing beat of club music as they pass by.

"Wow." Darryn clears his throat, sounding as unnerved as I feel. "Is that what yesterday was like?"

I shake my head. "I mean, yeah, there was a lot of skin, but it was, like, shorts and tank tops." The next parade unit is led by a huge arch of rainbow-colored balloons, and I point at the screen. "Mostly it was more like this. Rainbows everywhere. Lots of colorful people. Art and food and things like that."

From the corner of my eye, I see Darryn nod. "Sounds fun."

"And exhausting," I add with a short laugh. "I thought my feet were going to fall off before we got back last night. We must've walked twenty miles."

"Ouch." Darryn winces but leans closer to the screen. "Is it over already? Looks like a bunch of motorcycle cops or something."

I glance back over as the credits start to roll. "Damn. Yeah, I guess it is. Sorry you missed most of it. Maybe next year we can—"

I cut that thought off, and an uncomfortable silence falls between us. Grasping for a new topic, I blurt out, "How are things with Rich?"

I hold back a wince. Not the best opening gambit, but it's out there now. I'll just have to work with it.

Darryn rolls his chair a few feet away. "It's going fine. Why do you ask?"

And here we go. "I'm just... Well, I was talking to Annie and Mo the other day, and they said a few things that made me worry. About how Rich treats you."

Darryn stares at me. "What's wrong with how Rich treats me?"

I chew my bottom lip. "He just... He hovers. He's always at practice now, watching you, and everyone who comes close to you. And then the way he grabbed your arm the other day..."

Darryn stands up, the move pushing his chair away so that it bumps into his desk. "It's fine," he protests, one hand coming up to rub at the spot where Rich grabbed him. "He's just high-strung sometimes. He apologized for that."

I'm only half listening by then. My eyes are glued to Darryn's arms. He's got his fingers wrapped around his right biceps, giving me a perfect view of the purple ring of bruises around his left wrist.

"Did he do that?"

Darryn's head pops up and he stares at me. "What?"

"That!" I point at the bruises. "Did he do that to you?"

Darryn glances down and then moves his arm out of my line of sight. "I told you, it's nothing. We were playing around." His voice is practically a growl. "My relationship with Rich is none of your business."

"It is if he's *hurting* you!" I'm on my feet then, my laptop shoved aside, tinny post-parade sounds still streaming from the speakers. He's making excuses and getting all defensive, like Mo said he might. "You're supposed to be my best friend, and you think that I'll ignore—"

"You're just jealous." In contrast to mine, Darryn's voice is flat. Toneless. "You're angry that I'm dating Rich instead of you, and you're taking it out on him."

I throw my hands up in the air in frustration. "This is not just about me being jealous. This is about you showing up with bruises that your so-called *boyfriend* gave you. This is about being your *friend*, Darryn."

"Some *friend* you are!" Darryn's on his feet and yelling now, too. "You think if you split us up that I'd come running to you and you'd get everything you want!"

"Do you think I wanted *any* of this?" The words tear at my throat, violent and painful. "Do you think I'm *enjoying* this? I have to see you with *him*. See you and know you're with *him* and not with *me*."

My voice cracks and breaks, and I have to bite my lip hard to hold back the sob that wants to follow my words. The sheen in Darryn's eyes shows he's hurting, too, but I don't have the energy to spare for his pain.

"And then *this*." I point at his arm. "He's hurting you. He's cutting you off from your friends, and now he's hurting you, and you won't listen to me because you think, 'oh, he's just jealous.'" I'm shaking from a near-lethal mix of anger, fear, and frustration. "Damn right I'm jealous, but that's not what this is about. He's an asshole, Darryn. And I can't stand here and listen to you defend his sorry ass."

"Grant—"

"No!" I'm done listening to his excuses. "It's over. It's done." I grab my backpack and laptop and head for the door, where I stop long enough to throw my parting shot over my shoulder.

"You made your bed. Go fuck in it."

Chapter Seven

I don't see Darryn for the next two days. I'm torn between residual anger, remorse, and worry. Losing my temper like that helped no one, and all it did, apparently, was drive Darryn right into Rich's arms—and his apartment. Where Rich could be doing anything to him, and no one would know.

Studying is impossible. My focus is shot to hell. All I can do is replay Sunday afternoon in my mind and wish I'd done or said something different. Something that would've gotten through to Darryn.

By Wednesday morning, short on sleep and long on regret, it takes all my effort to drag myself out of bed, shower and throw on some clothes, and head to class by way of the campus coffee shop. A gigantic vat of caffeine gets me through the morning, and I pick up a sandwich from the dining hall on my way back to the room, hoping to grab a nap before heading back out for practice.

I can hear voices before I even get to the door. Darryn's is as familiar as my own by now, but Rich's is louder, more strident. *They're fighting?* I try not to give in to the little cheer that rises in my chest at the thought. I mean, yeah, I'd be thrilled if Darryn dumped the fucking asshole.

That doesn't mean I want him to be hurt by it.

I stop outside the door, hesitant to interrupt what might be a breakup scene before the breaking up part is over, though that leaves me eavesdropping outside, and that's not cool, either. Then the words I'm hearing coalesce.

"…told you, you need to move out of here. I see the way he watches you!"

"Rich." Darryn's voice is placating, almost pleading. "He's my teammate and my friend. And you know the athletic department requires me to live in the dorm until I'm a junior."

"Screw that," Rich shoots back. "Your *friend* can tell Housing you're still here to keep them in the dark. It's final, babe. You're moving in with me."

I swallow back the gasp, barely. Not just at Rich's demand, but at the fact that it is a *demand*. He's past the point of asking now. He's telling Darryn how things are going to be.

The problems with eavesdropping forgotten, I lean closer and wait to hear Darryn's response.

"I told you I'm not ready for that, even if I could move off campus." He raises his voice and talks faster. "And I'm not looking for another roommate, either. I already spend most of my time with you when I'm not in class or at practice. I'm not giving up my closest *friend*"—he emphasizes the word, as if underlining the platonic nature of our relationship—"and I'm not moving. Not in with you, and not to another room in the dorms."

Rich's next words come out in a growl. "You don't get how this works."

There's a pause and then Darryn voice comes through. "Rich…*stop*."

I don't like the sound of that.

I scramble to get my keys out of my pocket and into the lock, not even trying to listen to whatever it is Rich is ranting about now. The door finally gives, and I shove it open just in time to see Rich grab Darryn by the wrist—the same one he'd already left bruised. In two strides, I grab Rich's arm and wrench him off Darryn.

Rich turns toward me, fury written all over his face and his free hand curling into a fist. I duck to miss his swing, years of gymnastics training giving me the speed and flexibility to get the hell out of the way. Before I can do anything else, though, Darryn's there, way too close, and when Rich spins back to face him, his arm slams into Darryn's shoulder. A second later, Darryn hits the wall with a yelp of pain.

Rich takes a step back, toward me, and I don't even think. I grab his arm with both hands and yank, using his momentum and my upper body strength to slingshot him right through the open doorway and into the hall. If he bounces off the doorframe a little in the process, I'm not about to give a shit.

I kick the door shut, flip the lock, and turn all my attention to Darryn.

He's shivering and whimpering a little, and his right shoulder looks grotesque under his T-shirt. Dislocated, *fuck*. Anyone's who's been doing gymnastics as long as we have could tell that in a second. He's got his left wrist cradled in his lap, too, and it's more than a bruise this time. From the way it's swelling, I'm hoping it's not broken.

My brain snaps to attention finally, and I dig my phone out of my pocket as I crouch in front of Darryn. "It's gonna be okay," I murmur while dialing 911. "We're gonna get you taken care of."

Vaguely, I register that Rich has recovered enough to yell through the door, though I don't spare the energy to try to make out the words. I've got a dispatcher on the line already, and I'm giving her the quick and dirty on Darryn's injuries and where to find us.

There's a loud *bang* as I finish up and the door shakes in its frame. "And the guy who started this is still raging in the hallway outside, so you might want to send some cops to deal with him, too."

"Please stay on the line, sir." The dispatcher's voice is sharper then, but I keep my focus on Darryn. He's looking up at me from under his eyelashes, eyes pinched with pain, fear lurking behind.

"No cops," he whispers. "I don't want..."

He doesn't finish the thought, but I can bet on what's coming. He doesn't want to press charges. "Fuck that," I whisper back harshly. "Bury the fucker under charges and send him to jail."

"No!" Darryn tries to lean forward for emphasis but cries out again and slumps back against the wall. "He didn't mean to—"

"He hurt you!" I don't even care anymore what the dispatcher or anyone outside might hear. I can't believe he can still defend that asshole. "I don't care if he meant to! If you think I'm not going to make sure he pays for it—watch me."

I can feel the anger radiating off Darryn like heat waves in the desert. I'm immune. He's here with me, not with that asshole, and his obvious injuries aside, he's mostly in one piece. Nothing else matters.

A preternatural calm settles over me. "Hate me if you have to." I settle in as close to him as I can get without touching him. "Hell, I can live with you hating me for the rest of your life. As long as it's a long, happy, and safe life."

Darryn clams up after that, and he keeps his head turned away.

That's all right. He's safe, and that's enough.

• • •

The next hour is a blur. Both campus security and the cops arrive, and it turns out—as I learn later—the RA and a couple of other guys who live on the hall, including Pace, held onto Rich when he finally realized he might be in trouble and tried to run. I leave Darryn's side only long enough to unlock the door for the paramedics, who mention resetting Darryn's shoulder before they move him but reconsider when I ask how that'll affect his gymnastics.

They won't let me ride in the ambulance with him, and I can't even think of driving myself, so Pace gives me a lift to the hospital. He's still sitting next to me in the waiting room, and I'm clutching my phone in one hand like a lifeline, when Darryn's parents arrive. I stand and wait for them to talk to the intake desk before walking over.

"Mr. and Mrs. Kaneko."

Mrs. Kaneko turns first. She doesn't smile, but that doesn't surprise me, considering the circumstances. They've always been perfectly cordial to me when I've been around them—they even had me over for dinner a couple of times back in the spring—but she's never seemed to be the smiling type, and she certainly doesn't have much reason to smile now.

"Grant," she says. "Have you seen him?"

I shake my head. "Not family. They wouldn't let me go back with him. He's okay, though," I hurry to reassure them as best I can. "I mean, he didn't pass out or anything like that."

Mr. Kaneko is facing me now, too. "What happened?" he asks, and I realize they know their son is injured, not that it happened because his boyfriend—ex-boyfriend, dammit—is a massive asshole.

"I can't…" I don't know what to tell them. I have no idea

if they know he's dating someone at all, much less a man. I can't risk outing him like that.

"I think Darryn should tell you the whole story," I finally manage. "He might not want to, though." I feel I should warn them. "I mean, it's... He might be...embarrassed?" That's not quite the word I'm looking for, but it'll have to do.

Mr. and Mrs. Kaneko look thoroughly confused in addition to the concern now, but they'll be talking to their son soon enough. "Um, if you could tell him I'm here?" I shrug. "I'd like to see him if they'll let me go back."

Mrs. Kaneko's mouth softens into the closest to a smile that I've seen from her. "You were with him when it happened?"

I nod. "Yeah. I couldn't do much, but I called 911."

She reaches out and touches my arm, the softest brush of her fingertips. "We'll tell him you're here."

A nurse calls their names then, and they turn and follow her down the hallway. I return to my seat and tilt my head back against the wall while I wait.

I'll wait however long it takes to know that he's going to be okay.

I don't know how long I've been sitting with my mind blank when suddenly a hand touches my shoulder.

"Grant."

I jerk upright and focus on the face in front of me. Annie.

"Hey." My voice sounds like I've been gargling glass.

Annie holds out a bottle of water. "Drink," she orders, and I do.

After a few swallows, I hand the bottle back. "What are you doing here?"

"Mo called me." She takes the seat next to me. "Some kind of grapevine at U of A, I gotta say." She pauses. "Which means I don't know exactly what happened, just that the police showed up and Darryn got taken off to the hospital.

Was it Rich?"

I shrug. "You and Mo were right about him."

She winces. "Not the kind of thing I like being right about. How is he?"

I tip my head back and stare up at the ceiling. "Don't know. I mean, he's got a messed-up shoulder and wrist, but I think he'll be fine. Physically, at least."

Annie sighs. "Mentally?"

"Who knows?" I roll my head to the side to look at her. "I don't think telling him he's better off without that rat bastard is going to be a lot of help."

"He'll figure it out." Annie reaches over to take my hand. "Give him time."

Time.

I try not to think about how much time he might need to be okay again.

Chapter Eight

I haven't the faintest idea what time I stumbled back into the dorm room and fell onto my bed after the hospital pushed us out the door in the wee hours. I would've thought there was no way I could sleep after all that, but the adrenalin crash hit me hard. I vaguely remember silencing my normal eight a.m. alarm. When my eyes open for good, though, it's to bright sunshine and the low battery warning pinging from my cell phone.

I fumble for the phone and squint at the screen. 11:23.

Well.

Guess I won't be making it to classes today.

I plug in my phone to charge and then sleepwalk my way through a shower to scrub off the inevitable antiseptic smell that lingers from the hospital. For once, the communal bathroom is deserted, and I'm glad for it. Last thing I need is to run into anyone asking questions about last night. And you can bet the whole school knows the story by now.

Back in the room, I pull a bottle of water out of the minifridge and sit on the edge of the bed while I drain it in one long pull. Dry throat banished, I consider lunch. Food would probably be a good idea, although all I really want to do is go back to the hospital and sit by Darryn's bedside.

I'd do it in a heartbeat if I thought it wouldn't make things even more awkward.

I can't face the dining hall yet—I can't face *people* yet—so I scrounge through the emergency snack drawer in my desk and come up with a bag of chips and some trail mix. Not exactly gourmet, but it'll have to do.

My phone buzzes, and I lunge for it with the hope that maybe it's Darryn.

Nope. Annie. *You awake yet?*

Barely, I reply.

Before I can type a follow-up text, the phone starts ringing. I sigh and answer with a "hey."

"Hey." Annie's voice sounds as rough as mine. "I just got off the phone with Mom. She said she tried to call you, but you didn't answer."

"I was asleep," I remind her. "What's up?"

Annie blows out a breath. "Apparently the news got the story. Not a lot of detail, just that the cops got called and a student got arrested for assaulting another one. No names or anything. She wanted to check on us."

Great. After repeating the story at least four or five times last night, including to three different cops, I'd been hoping to get through a day without going over it again. It's bad enough that I have the memory of Darryn hitting the wall and slumping to the floor, which my mind ever so helpfully keeps replaying in brilliant technicolor.

"What did you tell her?" Maybe Annie saved me the trouble.

"I told her you were fine and not in any trouble. I didn't want to tell her what happened and screw it up. I'm not clear on everything myself. She wants us to come home this weekend, probably so she can inspect us for herself."

My head starts pounding again. "Fine. We can do that."

Annie's quiet for a few seconds. "Do you want to call her, or should I?"

I cannot deal. "You. I can't…it's not that…"

"Got it." She sighs again. "I'll text her. Tell her we'll be there as soon as we can get away after classes and practice and whatever on Friday. And that we'll explain then."

"Yeah." I tilt over sideways until my head lands on my pillow. "I just can't deal today."

"I understand." She pauses again. "How about I bring over pizza for dinner? No conversation required. I'll even get your favorite."

"You hate pepperoni." It's a lifelong argument.

"I don't *hate* it. I just don't *love* it. I can always pick it off."

I'm going to owe her big time the next time she's going through a life crisis. "With root beer?"

"Of course, silly. I'll be over at six. Try to be marginally presentable by then, okay?"

She ends the call before I can respond, but that's fine because I'm about halfway back to sleeping anyway. Before I let myself drift away, though, I set an alarm for five. I don't think I'll sleep all afternoon, but stranger things have happened.

• • •

The pounding on my door sounds muffled. The reason becomes clear when I open it and find Annie standing on the other side with a pizza box in one hand and a loaded plastic bag in the other. She must have knocked with her foot.

"Here." She shoves the pizza box at me and shifts the bag to her right hand and shakes out her left. "Bag was cutting off the circulation."

I snort and spin on one heel. "C'mon in. I even have a roll of paper towels."

"I did grab some napkins," Annie replies as she pushes the door shut behind her. "Those things never hold up well to pizza grease."

"Truth." I set the pizza box on my desk and pull Darryn's chair over, doing my best to drag my mind away from him at the same time. Annie adds two bottles of Barq's and follows those up with a six-pack of chocolate-frosted doughnuts. I side-eye her for that last one.

"Are you trying to fatten me up? I'm in training, you know."

She blows a raspberry. "One doughnut won't kill you. I'll leave the rest in the TV room. They'll last about two seconds there."

"If that." I flip open the pizza box and pull loose a slice. Annie follows suit, and we finish the first few bites before she speaks up again.

"So. You and Darryn."

I shake my head as I swallow. "There is no me and Darryn."

"But you want there to be."

I take a sip of root beer while I figure out how to dodge that one. "Darryn's not...he doesn't..."

Annie snorts. "He does." She takes another bite and watches my reaction.

I fold like an umbrella. "He did," I admit, picking at a slice of pepperoni. "I screwed it up."

"As you do." Annie tosses down the remains of her crust and reaches for her root beer. "What did you do?"

I shrug one shoulder. "Didn't trust him enough to come out to him."

Annie chokes on her soda. "Wait. You didn't come out to me until we were eighteen. You still haven't come out to our parents. Pretty sure Darryn and Mo are the only other people who know at all."

"Yeah, but…" I blow out a breath. "I didn't actually *tell* him. He figured it out. He was waiting for me to tell him." I shake my head. "I never did. And he decided that meant I didn't trust him."

"Oh." Annie's head of steam deflates.

"Yeah. Oh." I drop my second slice of pizza back in the box, untouched. My appetite's gone, my stomach too busy twisting to digest. My head's not doing much better. It feels even worse when I say all that out loud.

Annie reaches for a napkin. "I guess I get why he came to a conclusion like that. But he forgot one kind-of-big thing."

I poke at a bit of cheese. "What's that?"

Annie pokes *me* until I look her way. "He never told *you*, either."

I can only shrug in response. "Yeah, I thought of that." Like, only a thousand times since then. "But he was just figuring out that he liked guys. I've known for a while. I should've told him a year ago. Now he's mad. Probably doesn't even want to see me."

Annie leans back against the wall, staring at me. "Wow. You're really shooting for the depths of despair, aren't you?"

The sound that leaves my throat would never be confused for an actual laugh. "Yeah, well, it's dark and quiet down here and nobody expects anything of me. I'm thinking I'll just hang out here for a while."

"Well, fuck that noise." Annie smacks my shoulder with the back of her hand. "Get that bullshit out of your system and pull yourself together. Sooner, not later."

I stare at her. "Why does it matter?"

She grabs my chin in one hand. "Because you aren't going to do anyone any good soaking in your own self-pity. And by *anyone*, I mean *Darryn*."

I jerk my head away from her grip. "That's a low blow."

"Nope." She picks up her pizza. "I think it's exactly at the right height." She wiggles the slice in my direction. "Unless you'd rather I slap you across the face with this? I hear pepperoni is great for your skin."

I push her hand away. "All right, I get the point." I reach for my abandoned pizza slice. "Is it okay with you if I wallow a little longer? I haven't even gotten a full day in yet."

Annie grins around her bite. "One night," she agrees. "Tomorrow, it's back to real life. Warts and assholes and all."

I snort. "Can we keep talk of warts separate from talks of assholes?"

"Gross. And deal."

She pokes me in the ankle with her toe. I retaliate by trapping her foot between mine, and within seconds, we're in a full-fledged foot war, laughing like the idiots we are.

This right here? This is why she's here tonight. And I love her for it.

· · ·

I try to let everything go that night. I do. But I sleep for crap, and the whole next day feels like swimming through oatmeal. My brain's foggy, my body's sort of achy, and by the time I hit the gym for practice, I'm about ready to curl up on a mat and pull my hoodie over my head.

"Clark!"

First, time to pay the piper for missing yesterday's practice.

I head over to where Coach Everson's waiting for me. He doesn't have literal steam coming out of his ears, so that's a good sign.

I stop in front of him. "Sorry, Coach. I don't have an excuse."

He lifts an eyebrow. "That's not what I heard."

I blink in surprise before my sluggish brain catches up. Of course he knows what happened. Even if he hadn't heard through the school's official channels, gossip runs through this place like wildfire. Hell, he probably knew by the time we got Darryn to the hospital.

"I still should've—"

"Yeah, you should have, but extenuating circumstances." He claps me on the shoulder. "Regular practice today, but I want you working with Kenny again next week."

I can't imagine having enough concentration for that so soon. On the other hand, that's probably the point—give me something to focus on besides whatever's going on with Darryn. I nod. "Yes, Coach."

"Okay. Get to work."

I nod again and head for the locker room, ready to hit the mats—instead of a mattress—and leave everything else behind for a little while.

Well, as much as I can without Darryn there beside me.

Suited up, I get to work, following Coach Sato's direction to the floor exercise. I'm pretty sure that's a calculated decision. In my current state, putting me anywhere above ground level is likely to end in nothing good.

Once I'm warmed up, I run through my routine, knowing it's nothing close to my best but just glad to make it all the way to the end without wiping out. Coach Sato meets me at the edge of the mat, his gaze far too probing, but he's gentler than I deserve.

"Not bad. You've got all the moves in place. If you can get that last tumbling pass nailed down, we might try working in more difficulty."

I'm surprised at that, but I give yet another nod. I'm starting to feel like a bobblehead. "Maybe another twist on the second run? There's more to work with there."

"Maybe." Coach claps me on the shoulder. "Right now, go through it again. Hit it harder this time."

"Yes, Coach."

I go through the exercise twice more before Coach sends me over to the high bar. I guess they figure with a spotter and double mats, I can't damage myself too much there.

Seems they're right. I only slip once, and I land on my feet. How metaphorical.

By the time I head for the locker room after focusing on my body for a couple of hours, my head's in a better place. Not clear, but less muddy. It's something, I suppose.

. . .

Annie drags me home that weekend—literally. She's at my dorm room when I get there after practice Friday afternoon, and she grabs my arm and doesn't let go until she shoves me into the front seat of our car. I grumble, but she turns on the radio—"driver picks the music, shotgun shuts his cakehole"— and concentrates on the mess otherwise known as Atlanta traffic.

I spend the trip staring at my phone. I've texted Darryn three times, just trying to check in. I haven't gotten a response. I hope that means he's spending his energy on recovery, and not that he's actively avoiding me. Either way, I don't want to bug him too much.

I still really, *really* wish he'd at least let me know he's doing okay.

After thirty minutes, Annie pulls into our driveway, turns off the car, and blows out a breath. "Okay. Just the facts, no discussions of anyone's sexuality, eat dinner, and then back to campus. Deal?"

I clear my dry throat. "Deal."

She gets out, and I shove my phone into my pocket as I

follow her up to the porch. The front door opens as we climb the steps.

Dad greets us with a big smile. "The wanderers have returned!"

Annie rolls her eyes but steps into the hug he offers. "Not like we've been off exploring the world, Dad. We're fifteen miles away."

"It only feels like more because we never see you." Dad lets her go and opens his arms to me. For just a few seconds, soaking up that hug, I feel like a kid again, with my parents standing like a shield between me and all the bad things out there.

It's harder to let go than I'd like to admit, and I follow Annie into the house.

"Come on in, kids, dinner's ready!" Mom's voice comes from the kitchen, so we head in that direction, only to meet her halfway in the dining room. She's got a bowl of salad in her hands, and the table already holds a pan of lasagna and a smaller one of garlic bread. Annie makes a happy little sound—it's one of her favorite meals—and takes her usual seat at the table while simultaneously reaching for her plate and the big spoon sticking out of the pan.

We go through the usual process of serving our plates, but as soon as we're all settled, Mom asks the question. "What's all this that happened, Grant?"

My first bite of lasagna lands in my stomach like lead. I focus on my plate while I tell her, in as few words as I can manage. "Darryn was friends with this guy who turned out to be…well, abusive, I guess. They argued in our room and Rich knocked Darryn into the wall. It was an accident"—as much as it pains me to admit, it's the truth—"but he still sprained his wrist and dislocated his shoulder."

I take in a deep breath, trying not to relive what happened. Just talking about it is bad enough. I don't need to go back over every detail again. And definitely not in front of my parents, who are still missing a big piece of the story.

"Oh my goodness." Mom reaches out to lay a hand over mine. "Is he going to be okay?"

I push back the question of whether *I'm* okay and give her a tiny smile. "He should be. I didn't see him after we got to the hospital, but his dad told me he was okay. I mean, it'll take him a while to heal. But he'll be okay."

"That's terrible." Dad's frowning face, brow furrowed, is exactly what I expected to see. "Did they arrest the other boy?"

"Yeah," Annie breaks in. "That's how I found out what was going on. I heard the sirens, and then our friend Mo called and told me to get over to Grant's dorm. I saw them put someone in a police car. I didn't know for sure it was Rich until I got to the hospital."

I stare at her. She hadn't told me that much detail. But then, I hadn't asked. My only concern was to make sure Darryn got the help he needed. Rich could fall off the face of the earth for all I cared.

"Oh my. Poor Darryn." Mom squeezes my hand. "I hope the school is doing something about it. That bully should be expelled."

I don't have any answers to give her. I cut off another tiny bite of lasagna, then set down my fork. The way my stomach is roiling, I don't dare try to eat it.

Annie saves me. "I'm sure they're working on all that, since it happened in the dorm," she says. "They'll make sure it's all taken care of."

"Good," Dad replies. His gaze on me makes me want to squirm. One of those parental specialties, I guess. I do my best to ignore it. I never have been a good liar. I never got in too much trouble when I was growing up, but I still get caught in half-truths and omissions an embarrassing number of times. If I say anything more now, I'm likely to spit out the rest of the story. And I'm absolutely *not* ready to come out to my parents right now.

Annie reads me, again. "Anyway, that's the big news of the week." She almost sounds normal, even. "Usually the most excitement on campus is when the dining hall sets up the banana split bar."

That forces a snort of a laugh out of me, and the tension around the table drops by about a thousand percent. Annie grins and launches into a story about two guys in one of her computer classes almost coming to blows over Mac versus PC, and the rest of us go back to our dinners. My appetite is still MIA, but I force myself to eat a reasonable amount before I set down my fork and finish my tea. Mom's finished by then, too, so I stand and reach for her plate and mine.

"You don't have to do that, dear," Mom starts to object, but I shake my head.

"You cook, we clean up," I tell her. "Them's the rules."

I take the plates into the kitchen, and I've just finished scraping and rinsing them for the dishwasher when Annie joins me carrying her plate and Dad's. "Buttering them up for more revelations?"

I shake my head violently as I slide the first two plates into the dishwasher rack. "Nope. I've had enough emotional exposure for one night."

Annie finishes scraping her plates, but when she hands them over for me to rinse, she pauses and catches my gaze. "You know they aren't going to mind."

I stare at her, biting my lip, then nod. "Rationally, yeah, I know. Tell my rampant teenage anxiety that."

Annie rolls her eyes and lets go of the plates. "We'll be twenty in May," she points out. "No more blaming the teen years or the hormones."

"Sure," I tell her as I turn toward the sink. "No problem.

Piece of cake."

She smacks my arm. "Doofus."

I respond with a hip-check. "Dork."

Some things will never change, no matter how old we get. It's a strangely comforting thought.

Of course, there are downsides to being a twin. We might not have actual telepathy—it sure would be helpful if we did—but we're pretty darn good at reading each other's moods.

"Still haven't heard from Darryn?"

I wince as I scrub at a stubborn bit of baked-on cheese on the edge of the lasagna pan. "Nope."

"Have you called him?"

"Also nope." I turn to slide the pan into the dishwasher.

"Why not?"

I don't have a good answer for that one. I shrug. "He hasn't answered my texts."

"Duh." Annie smacks my shoulder lightly. "He injured his wrist. Might make it kind of hard to type, don't you think?"

I facepalm at myself. "I imagine it would." I drop my hand and give her a look. "I'll call him tomorrow. Promise."

"Good." Annie hands me the last two glasses. "Now let's get this finished up and go watch something mindless with the parents."

I laugh. "That sounds like the best idea I've ever heard."

Chapter Nine

I keep my promise. Sunday night, just before I head to bed, I call Darryn. It rings and rings, finally rolling over to voicemail. My throat closes up as I listen to Darryn's voice asking me to leave a message, but I manage to force out a few words.

"Hey," I say. "Just checking in to see how you're doing. I hope you're not in too much pain. Um." I swallow. "Take care of yourself."

I end the call before I start rambling. I lie on my bed staring at the ceiling, my traitorous brain playing and replaying the conflict with Rich and its aftermath, until I finally fall into a fitful sleep in the wee hours.

I'm dragging my tailfeathers when I get to the gym Monday afternoon. Coach Everson doesn't waste a second when I walk in.

"Clark!" he yells. "Get dressed out and hit the floor. You're with Washington today."

I muster up as much energy as I can to reply. "Sure thing, Coach!" I head toward the locker room, nodding toward a few teammates as I pass them. I'm suited up within minutes and head back out. Kenny's already on the floor exercise mat warming up, so I join him, going through my usual pre-practice stretches.

Focusing on my body works its usual magic. By the time I'm ready to go, I'm feeling more alert, but my mind's quiet. *What happens outside the gym stays outside the gym.*

I turn toward Kenny, who's climbing to his feet from what I have to admit was a pretty impressive backbend. "You ready?"

Kenny nods and gives a tiny smile. "As I'll ever be."

I chuckle. "I doubt that." I step off the edge of the mat and wave one arm. "Let's see how you're doing. You want to run the whole routine or just that section?"

Kenny ponders for a second. "One run-through would probably be good."

"Okay then." I clap my hands. "Go for it."

I watch as Kenny moves to his starting spot, collects himself, and then spins into action, his routine starting with a pivot on one foot. He doesn't have a high difficulty level overall, but his moves are precise, each turn sharp, every landing stuck. When he gets to his flairs, they're executed properly and definitely improved from our last session, but he's still not getting the height he needs.

He finishes in a full split, his arms extended up in a perfect vee, and I clap twice as he relaxes and meets my gaze for a second before climbing up off the mat.

"Good job," I tell him as I walk over to him. "Your flairs look sharp, but you could still add some height. Don't give up any momentum as you go through them. Keep pushing from start to finish."

Kenny nods quickly before glancing up at me, biting his lip, and throwing me completely off balance. "I, um. I don't know if it's okay to ask." He keeps his voice low. "How's

Darryn? I haven't seen him back around campus yet."

I take in a quick breath. "He's okay," I say, hoping it's the truth. "He's at home for now so he has his parents to help him with stuff."

I stop there, and Kenny shifts from one foot to the other. "Are you two…um…"

My stomach clenches, but I hold in my instinctive reaction and shake my head. "No offense," I say, as gently as I can manage, "but that's none of your business."

Kenny's face falls, and I hold back the urge to apologize. I don't fault him for asking, but I'm here as his coach, not his friend. "Okay. Let's work on the flairs. You're doing much better." I add the last to assuage my residual, inexplicable guilt, though it's not a lie. He *is* getting better.

Kenny nods, so I wave toward the mat. "Start with that set of backflips that leads into the floor work. Go through it easy once and let me take a look, and then we'll work on the details."

I back off the mat to watch while Kenny pulls his mind back into the game, and then for the next half hour, I run Kenny through his paces, giving him tips and demonstrating a few moves. We adjust his approach to the flairs slightly to give him more momentum to carry through, and I make a mental note to check the change with Coach Everson. I'm supposed to be helping him with his routine, not changing it up.

After one more run-through of the floor work section, I nod as Kenny climbs up. He's got to be tired, which makes this a good time to go through the full routine. If he can handle it fatigued, he'll be much better equipped to handle the stress of competition.

"All right. Let's put it all together now."

"Yes, Coach." Kenny looks as surprised as I feel at his instinctive words, but I flash him a small smile and nod before he moves to his starting position. He takes a deep breath and then launches into his opening moves, and I blink, startled. I don't know if he'd been distracted before, wondering about Darryn, but he's hitting every point perfectly. His flairs are high and fully extended, and when he swings into the final split and lifts his arms over his head, he looks every inch an Olympic champion. I can't help breaking out into a grin.

"Nailed it!" He returns my grin before climbing up and bouncing on his toes once before walking toward me. I clap him on his shoulder when he reaches me, just like Coach Everson does when any of us has a good routine. "You've got that down for sure," I tell him. "Comes down to doing it over and over again until it comes naturally and you don't even have to think about it."

His smile slips and he looks down and away. "Thanks," he murmurs. "I mean…" He shrugs. "Thanks."

I squeeze his shoulder one more time and drop my hand away. "I think our time's about up." I glance toward the digital clock on the wall as Coach Everson blows his whistle.

"That's it, guys," he yells. "Time to hit the showers."

I shoot one last glance Kenny's way, but he doesn't look up, so I head toward the locker room. I feel a thousand percent better than I did on Friday. I'm actually pretty proud of myself. I'm still worried about Darryn, and I still miss him, but I managed to set that all aside and focus on my goal—coaching. The session went well, and I really feel like I helped Kenny.

I'll keep trying to get in touch with Darryn, of course. In the meantime, life has to go on.

• • •

Tuesday and most of Wednesday pass in a near-normal blur of classes, meals, and homework. I almost don't notice the gaping hole on the other side of the dorm room, though I can't say my sleep is anything to write home about. I send one more text message, but I leave it at that. If Darryn wants to get in touch with me, he knows how to reach me.

I get to practice Wednesday a few minutes late, thanks to a long-running lecture in my last class, so I hurry through getting changed and jog out onto the gym floor. When I make it out, though, Coach Everson blows his whistle and waves an arm.

"C'mon, guys, gather 'round."

I join the others in a loose half circle, facing him and Coach Sato, who stands with his arms crossed across his chest, face neutral. I can't decide if that's good news or bad.

"All right, guys," Coach Everson says. "It's a small campus. I know you've all heard about what happened to Kaneko last week."

I can't help it; I jerk in surprise, and I can see several guys cut their eyes in my direction before dragging their attention back to Coach, who's still talking.

"I talked to Kaneko's parents a few hours ago, and they asked me to pass along some information. Kaneko—Darryn," he corrects himself at that point. "Darryn is doing well. He has a second-degree sprain of his left wrist, and his right shoulder was dislocated."

He pauses and shakes his head. "I don't know yet how this is going to affect him in here, in the gym, but that's not my primary concern, and it shouldn't be yours, either. He's healing, but he's got a long road ahead of him. And he's going to need all the support we can give him."

Murmurs of agreement come from around me. I'm still frozen in place, glued to Coach's every word. How is he really doing? And when is he coming back?

"It looks like Darryn might finish up this semester from home." It's as if Coach read my mind. "They're still working out those details. I told Mr. Kaneko that if there's anything we can do, we'll be happy to help." He pauses and glances around at us. "And when he *does* make it back here, the whole team will be here to help, too."

"Yeah!"

That comes from Heath, and it surprises laughs out of several others. Coach flashes a brief, small smile. "Okay." He claps his hands together. "Now let's get to work."

I bite back the million other questions I want to ask. Like, why the hell couldn't Darryn tell me any of that himself?

I need to get out of my head, and putting my body through its paces is just the ticket.

A few hours later, muscles still burning from practice, I'm in the corner of the dining hall, picking at what's left of my lukewarm spaghetti, when someone bumps my shoulder.

"Wake up, bro." Annie takes the seat across from me. "Faceplanting into your pasta might seem like a good idea. The mess? Not so great."

I give her what I know is an anemic smile. "Kind of a blah day, I guess."

Annie frowns as she sprinkles a packet of parmesan onto her own pile of pasta. "Still haven't heard from Darryn?"

I give up on eating and shove my tray aside. "Not directly. Coach Everson gave us an update at practice today. He's doing okay, recuperating at home."

Annie snorts softly. "The 'resting comfortably' line. How helpful."

I fold my arms on the table and tuck my shoulders up toward my ears. "It's better than no word at all."

I'm aware of how petulant I sound. Annie doesn't press, but I find myself talking anyway.

"I keep hoping to get a call, or a text, or a freaking snail-mail letter—some kind of word. I've sent him several texts, and I even called once, but I got voicemail. I don't want to annoy him, but I don't even know if he hasn't gotten the messages or if he doesn't want to talk to me."

When everything went down with Rich, all I could think of was making sure Darryn was okay, even if he hated me for it. But never thought he actually would.

Now I'm not so sure.

Annie sets down her fork and reaches across to tap her finger on my arm. "Give him some time," she tells me. "He's probably still in pain, and I don't just mean physically. He's got a lot to work through."

I know she's right. That doesn't make things easier.

"Thanks." I roll my shoulders and then stand and reach for my tray. "Got a test in anthro tomorrow and I'm a chapter behind. I better get to it."

Annie shudders. "Glad I got that out of the way last year. I'd offer to help, but the last thing I want to do is relive it."

I snort. "You stick with the computers, I'll handle the humanity."

"Deal." Annie shoots me a grin that's only about half the usual, but it's something, at least.

I head for the door, dropping off my tray along the way, and try to focus my thoughts on what I need to review tonight. It's impossible not to think of Darryn, though, especially with all the study sessions we'd shared over the past year. I could use a study bet right about now to keep me focused.

More than that, though, I'd love to have my best friend back.

Pretty sure my focus is going to be shot until I hear from Darryn.

If I hear from Darryn.

• • •

I survive my anthropology test, the rest of my classes, and

three more afternoons of practice before the weekend stretches out in front of me, endless and empty. I have a paper and another big test coming up the next week, but the idea of hanging out in my suddenly solo dorm room and trying to study leaves me cold. The library isn't a better prospect, exactly, but at least I'm less likely to feel like the walls are closing in on me.

Library it is.

I find a spot deep in the stacks, and I'm an hour into research on my paper when my cell phone rings. *Crap.* I forgot to set it to vibrate. I ignore the heads turning my way and silence the ringtone as quickly as I can. When I see the name on the display, I freeze.

It's Darryn.

I swipe to answer, uncaring of the rules against phone calls in the library. "Hey." I keep my voice as low as I can.

"Grant?"

My heart drops. It's not Darryn after all. It's his dad.

"Hi, Mr. Kaneko. Is…is everything okay?"

"Yes. Darryn's doing well." There's a brief pause. "I wanted to call to say thank you."

My throat closes up, and it's all I can do to whisper, "Thank me?"

"For what you did for Darryn." Mr. Kaneko's voice is a strange combination of gentle and stilted. "I—we—are thankful that you were there to help him. We didn't…" He pauses again. "We didn't know about this…boy he was seeing. We didn't know—"

He stops short, but I can fill in the rest. They didn't know he was dating anyone, much less that it was a guy.

"I'm…I'm glad I could be there." It's the understatement of the century, but it's all I can manage to say. "I'm glad he's doing okay. I mean…he is doing okay, isn't he?" *Please tell me he doesn't hate me.*

"He is doing well," Mr. Kaneko repeats. "I know you've called to talk to him. He hasn't been ready to talk to anyone yet. I think...I think he will be soon. I think he'll want to talk to you first."

Relief floods through me. "Please tell him he can call or text any time he wants." I hope he knows that, but I want to be sure.

"I will." There's another brief pause. "Thank you again. We all owe you a debt of gratitude."

Take care of Darryn for me. "I...you're welcome," I say instead.

"Goodbye, Grant."

"Bye."

The calls ends, and I'm left sitting at my table, books spread out around me, staring at the phone in my hand. I close my eyes and picture Darryn's face.

Please call soon, I tell the mental image. *I miss you.*

Chapter Ten

The first text from Darryn comes three days later.

I'm sitting on my bed with my laptop out, trying to get through a rough draft of my paper, when my phone buzzes. I glance over and jolt when I see Darryn's name on the screen.

I pick up the phone and open the text.

Hard to text with one wrist in a splint and the other arm in a sling.

My heart's pounding and there's a swooping in my stomach as I consider my response. Darryn beats me to it.

I'd kill for a shower right about now.

I force my brain away from the image of Darryn naked and wet as I type with shaking hands. *What, insurance won't pay for a gorgeous nurse to come give you private sponge baths?*

I wish. Its fumble with a cloth over the sink or let my mom wash my junk.

He inserts about six emoji after that, running the gamut from an embarrassed face to an eggplant to a vomiting face. I laugh out loud.

Yeah, I'd stick with the sink, I send before scrambling for something else to say. *Do they at least have you on the good drugs?*

I wait for his reply. *Percocet is my friend but I only get that at night. Otherwise its Advil and being very very still.*

I wince. *Tell me they're at least feeding you well.*

All my favorites. Think I'm gonna turn orange from all the mac and cheese. I keep telling mom I don't need anything special. I like what she usually makes.

Which, I know, is heavy on the traditional rice, fish, and vegetables of their Japanese heritage. Darryn's parents are second-generation Americans, but they've made a point of maintaining much of their cultural roots. Not that they haven't adapted to American habits. Darryn's dad grills out as much as any other suburban dad in the South. I've been the beneficiary.

Tell her that, I suggest. *Comfort food is different from favorite food.*

Yeah.

I wait for more, but it doesn't come. I wonder for a minute if I should leave him alone. Then the little blue dots appear that indicate a message in progress.

How's practice?

I shift in my seat, not at all sure how to approach this. From what little I've heard, it'll be another week or two before he even starts physical therapy. It could be months before he can tackle any of the apparatus.

It's practice, I type, slowly. *Lots of hanging off rings and bars. Choking on chalk dust. Coach Everson and Coach Sato playing good cop/bad cop.*

Sounds like heaven. A second message comes up seconds later. *I wish I could come watch.*

I blink at my screen. *Why don't you? I mean, if you really want to, there's no reason you can't.*

His response is slow to come. *Not ready.*

This whole laborious conversation is killing me. I want to be there with him, listening to him talk, watching his face, his body language.

Can you have company?

This reply takes even longer. *I'm not ready.*

Then: *Soon, though. I promise.*

My eyes burn as I type my response. *I'm gonna hold you to that.*

• • •

The texts keep coming at random intervals over the next few days. It takes me until halfway through day three to realize that he's sending them around my class and practice schedule, at times I'm available to talk. My heart aches, and I miss him even more.

I'm lying in bed around ten Sunday night, in my empty, quiet dorm room, too keyed up to fall asleep but too tired to do anything else. We have two days of classes left before Thanksgiving and all my assignments are done, so I don't even have homework to do.

My phone rings, making me jump. No one ever calls me but my mom, Annie, and the occasional telemarketer. I pick it up and see the name I most want to see. *Darryn.*

I almost drop the phone in my scramble to swipe to answer. "H-hey!" I blurt out.

Darryn's soft laugh answers me. "Hey."

His voice is as familiar to me as my own. Just hearing that one word has me awake and energized, as if I've touched a live wire.

With effort, I keep my voice low like Darryn's, as if talking too loudly might break the fragile connection. "How are you feeling?"

"Woozy." He sighs, and I hear the sound of fabric rustling as he shifts. I try not to think of him half dressed and curled up in bed. "Took my nightly drugs an hour ago. I'm a little loopy. But I couldn't fall asleep."

"Me either." I roll onto my side, cradling the phone between my ear and the pillow. "It's too quiet."

He lets out a soft laugh. "No roommate crowding your space and making annoying noises."

My smile is wholly involuntary. "No roommate telling me to stop goofing off and get back to studying."

Darryn sighs again. "I'd have to tell myself that, too. Can't concentrate on anything."

The last thing I want to do is bring back painful memories, but my curiosity gets the better of me. "What did you end up doing about school?"

He blows out a breath. "I'm on a kind of modified online program. Two of my classes were being taught online anyway, so they switched me to those, and I'm doing a home study thing for bio."

He had four classes, though. "And the last one?"

"We decided I should take an incomplete in chemistry. Kind of hard to do the labs for that, and since I'm taking only three classes next semester, that'll give me time to finish up that one."

Unspoken was the likelihood that he wouldn't have practice and meets filling his schedule like we usually did in the spring.

"That sucks," I say. "Let me know if you need any help with bio. I can send you lecture notes or whatever."

"Actually…" Darryn pauses. "I was thinking, if you'd like to…you might come over this weekend so we can study together. I know it's Thanksgiving, but I'm a chapter behind, and I need to get caught up so I can take the final on time. Otherwise I'll have to take another incomplete."

If I hadn't been wide awake before, I would be after that. The prospect of seeing Darryn live and in the flesh for the first time since everything happened has me buzzing from head to toe.

"Sure." I'm impressed at my ability to sound calm. "I can bring over all my notes, and we can go over what you missed. It'll be good review for me anyway."

"Great." He hesitates again. "Does three on Saturday work? You can stay for dinner. I'll see if Mom will make sushi."

I'd never been much of a sushi fan until I had his mom's homemade sushi the year before, the first time I went to Darryn's house. "You sure it's no trouble?" I know damn good and well making those delicious rolls isn't the easiest thing in the world.

"She'll love it." I can hear the smile in Darryn's voice, and it brings a matching smile to my face. "I'll text you if we need to change the time or anything. Unless you hear something, I'll see you Saturday?"

"I'll be there."

Chapter Eleven

"Yo, parental units!"

I can feel Annie rolling her eyes at me as she follows me through the front door Tuesday evening. It's such a relief to have a few days away from school that we were off campus less than an hour after Annie finished her last class. Five long days of freedom stretch out ahead of us.

I drop my backpack and duffel bag on the worn armchair nearest the door as Mom comes around the corner from the kitchen.

"Parental unit number one reporting for duty!" She smiles and holds out her arms, and I let her fold me into a hug. Standing there in the entryway with her arms around me, warm and safe in the home where I grew up, I want to spill all the secrets I've been holding back.

I don't. I will, of course. But not yet.

I step away and let Annie have her turn as Dad comes rambling up the hallway from the den. "Hey, Dad," I say, and Dad gives me a hug, too, in more of a back-slapping, stereotypical man-to-man way.

"I'm so glad to have you both home," Mom says, and this time I see Annie roll her eyes.

"It's not like we're on another continent, Mom," she says.

"You'd think you were, as rarely as you visit." Dad wraps one arm around Annie's shoulders and gives her a shaking squeeze. "I figured you'd at least be back to do laundry every couple of weeks."

The truth is easy to read beneath the joking tone. They miss having us around. And honestly, even when things are going great, sometimes I miss being here. I love having the freedom of living on campus, but it sure would be nice to have someone else handling the cooking and cleaning—and yeah, the laundry.

This whole adulting thing can suck it.

"Y'all go get your things put away and wash up," Mom says. "We'll have dinner in about fifteen minutes. Dear, will you set the table?"

Dad lets out a long-suffering sigh. "See? Ever since you two moved away I have to set the table *and* clean up."

I laugh as I pick up my bags. "Ahh, the real reason you miss having us around."

"The truth is out there!" Dad chuckles as he heads off into the dining room, and I wave Annie ahead of me down the hall toward our rooms. They're side by side, doors directly across from each other, with a shared bathroom between. The setup is entirely too reminiscent of all the reruns of *The Brady Bunch* we watched as kids—though we do have a toilet.

When I walk in, my room looks exactly the same as it always does, and the sight makes me feel ten years old again. Okay, well, it's cleaner than I kept it when I was ten years old. I toss my bags on the edge of the bed and cross to the bathroom, where I quickly relieve myself and wash my hands. A glance in the mirror tells me Dad will probably comment on my hair over dinner. It's definitely getting overgrown. If I let it go much longer, I might be forced into the ranks of the man-bunned. And like Mo and Annie said at Pride, no one wants to see that.

"Bathroom's free!" I yell as I head back into my room, pulling the door on my side closed behind me. Annie and I managed to make it through our teen years with only a few near misses on the shared bathroom front, so habits like locking and knocking are well ingrained.

I perch on the edge of my bed long enough to check my messages. Nothing from Darryn since yesterday's calls. I type out a quick text. *Back at the parents'. Looking forward to eating my weight in home-cooked meals.*

I shove my phone into my pocket before I head back downstairs, resisting the urge to ride down the rail like I've been known to do. Darryn's never far from my mind, which means neither is his injury, and while it's mostly affected me on a personal level, I do think of the team, too. The last thing we need is for me to do something silly and end up on the injured list.

I can imagine how Coach Everson would react to *that*.

I swing into the kitchen as Mom pulls a bubbling casserole dish full of homemade macaroni and cheese out of the oven. My favorite. "Pulled out the big guns, didn't you?"

Mom laughs and sets the dish on a potholder next to the stove. "And oven-fried chicken. Your dad just put the platter on the table."

"No sneaking a piece before we eat," Dad chimes in as he comes to fetch the mac and cheese. "Grant, why don't you get the tea?"

I nod and reach into the fridge for the ever-present gallon jug of sweet tea before following Dad to the table, which is fully laden with the chicken, mac and cheese, a bowl of green beans, a pan of rolls, and place settings for four. I'm weirdly homesick at the sight, considering I'm at home. Guess I'm wishing for the days when I was a carefree kid.

As the past few months have taught me, growing up isn't all it's cracked up to be.

Annie appears in the doorway. "Perfect timing! Didn't have to help one bit."

"That's okay, dear," Mom says as she joins us. "You and Grant can clean up after."

She and Dad laugh as Annie and I grumble, but we all sit down and dig in. We used to say a blessing before every meal, but at some point we got out of the habit. Mom and Dad still go to the same small Methodist church we did when I was a kid. These days, I think it's more out of habit and friendship than anything else. The church is more liberal than some but still more conservative than any of us are these days.

That's part of what worries me about coming out to them. We grew up spending every Sunday at church, and while I don't remember any diatribes against homosexuality, I've heard enough from other fronts to give me pause. As progressive as our parents have gotten over the years, neither Annie nor I know how they'll react to finding out neither of their kids is exactly straight. I hope it's not going to be a problem for them, but there's enough doubt to power a few butterflies.

I try not to worry about any of that and enjoy my family. I know how lucky I am to have them. We eat and talk, laugh and tell stories—some of them even true. Every so often, an offhand comment or mention of a friend results in Annie and me exchanging a significant look.

I'm also thankful that this year it's just us for Thanksgiving. We've spent a few years with some of our extended family, but most of them wouldn't take the news well at all. It's part of the reason we don't spend much time around them, in fact. These days, political discussions never turn out happy.

By the time we're done with dinner, my eyelids are

drooping. Between the carb overload and the relief of having some free time, I'm about ready to drop. I'm a dutiful son, though, so I help Annie clear the table and load the dishwasher.

"Dibs on the leftover mac and cheese," I say as I'm covering the casserole dish with foil.

Annie snorts. "There's enough left to feed an army. Pretty sure if you tried to eat it all, you'd spend the rest of the day praying to the porcelain god."

"Still called dibs!" I slide the leftovers into the fridge while Annie closes the dishwasher and starts it running. I turn to leave the kitchen, but Annie stops me.

"Hey," she says in a low voice. "Should we talk to them now? Or do you want to wait?"

I shake my head. "Not yet. Let's get through Thanksgiving dinner first. Just in case."

Annie tilts her head. "Still worried about what they're going to say?"

I shrug. "Mostly no…a little bit yes." The butterflies beat their wings a little harder in my stomach. "I know we should get it over with…"

"I get it." Annie gives me a small smile. "Take a couple more days as kids before we have to deal with adult conversations."

I huff out a small laugh. "Exactly." A yawn catches me off guard. "And now I think I'm going to go sleep for about twelve hours."

"Sounds like a plan," Annie replies. "I won't be far behind you."

I nod and head down the hall, pausing at the opening to the living room to toss off a wave at Mom and Dad. "I'm heading to my room," I tell them. "No promises on how long I might sleep. Call if you need me."

"Try not to need you," Dad shoots back, a traditional

call-and-response that makes us both smile.

"Night, dear." Mom smiles, too, and the deep, comforting feeling of home follows me down the hall and right into my dreams.

• • •

Thanksgiving has always meant the same thing at the Clark house—lasagna for dinner Wednesday night, rolling out of bed on Thursday just in time for the Macy's parade, and then some version of a turkey dinner. Somebody throws some canned cinnamon rolls in the oven, and we eat those with our coffee (milk when Annie and I were younger). Mom gets the turkey started during a commercial break, and Dad's responsible for the cornbread dressing and gravy, both from his grandmother's recipes. Sweet potato casserole, green beans, canned cranberry sauce, rolls, and lots of sweet tea round out the meal, and dessert is a pecan pie and an apple pie from a local bakery.

Since Mom and Dad handle the food, Annie and I get cleanup duty, but we also get first dibs on our favorite leftovers.

By the time we're finished putting the last of the food away and the dishwasher is humming softly, we're all ready for naps. Heck, Dad's already passed out in his recliner, and Mom's curled up on the sofa.

I glance over at Annie and raise an eyebrow. She nods in silent agreement. We're not going to disturb them now.

"Naptime," I murmur, and she and I head down the hall to our bedrooms.

• • •

It's after lunchtime on Friday when Annie and I get our nerve together and approach Mom and Dad for The Big Talk.

We've eaten turkey sandwiches and the last of the leftover veggies, sitting in front of the noon news, which Dad never misses. Once we're done, Annie and I take the empty plates to the kitchen, where we give each other one last fortifying look and head into the living room.

I sit on one end of the sofa and Annie on the other. "Dad, would you mind turning off the TV?" I start. "Annie and I have something we need to tell you."

Dad obliges—the news just ended anyway—and he tilts his head like he always does when he's confused or surprised, making him look like an inquisitive puppy. Mom leans forward in her chair, her expression closer to alarm. "I hope nothing is wrong at school? I mean, except for Darryn, of course."

I shake my head. "No, school is great," I try to reassure her, though it doesn't seem to make a difference. "This is a little more personal than that."

I pause then, gathering up the courage to say the words. Annie saves me the trouble.

"Grant's gay," she blurts out. "And I'm pretty sure I'm bi."

Nobody moves for about five seconds, and then Mom relaxes back into her chair. "Oh," she says. "Well...I'm not sure what to say? I'm happy for you both, and I'm glad that you told us."

Dad's head has tilted farther. "Okay, I get the gay part," he says. "I wondered, I mean. The way you are with Darryn?" He stops and straightens up. "It *is* Darryn, right?"

I start to nod but pause. "Well, kind of. I mean, I'm gay anyway. I'd be gay with or without Darryn in the picture."

"Right, right." Dad waves a hand, as if my sexuality's been a foregone conclusion. "But you like Darryn?"

I sigh. "Yes, Dad. I like Darryn. I told you he got hurt, but that wasn't the whole story." I take a deep breath. "He was seeing a guy who got pretty controlling. And then he got physical."

Dad sits up straight, and Mom covers her mouth. "This other boy is the one who hurt him?" Dad asks.

"Kind of. It was sort of an accident." I struggle with what to say next, but Annie jumps in to save me again.

"They were in their dorm room, and Grant got there and broke things up before it got any worse." She smiles at me. "Not all heroes wear capes."

I blush and duck my head. "Not a hero," I mumble. "Just glad I was in the right place at the right time."

Dad clears his throat. "That does change the picture of what happened. I assume the school and Darryn's parents are still taking care of things?"

I lift my head to give him a nod. "They're working on it. And Darryn will be okay, eventually. He's not in a good place for a relationship right now." Left unspoken is my greater fear. That even when he is ready, it won't be with me.

Dad frowns but lets the subject go, turning his attention to Annie. "And you, honey? You have your eye on someone?"

I don't know that I've ever seen Annie blush that deeply, and considering her pale skin, that's saying a lot. "Not… really," she stammers. "I mean, there are a…a few people I think are attractive, and…they aren't all guys. Not any one person or anything like that."

"Well." Dad sits back and flicks his gaze back and forth between us. "I can't say I'm completely surprised. I knew Grant and Darryn were…close. And Annie, you never seemed that interested in dating anyone."

Annie shrugs a shoulder. "Still not, really," she says. "It's mostly aesthetics at this point."

"And athletics." I flash her a grin when she sticks her tongue out at me.

Mom giggles. Actually *giggles*. "Well, I can't blame

anyone for admiring athletes. There are some very lovely ones to be admired."

"Mom!" Annie chokes on a laugh.

"She's not wrong," Dad chimes in. "But we'll save that discussion for another day. Right now, we've got a whole free afternoon ahead of us. How about we dig out the board games? Life? Clue? What's your poison, kids?"

Dad can be such a *dad* sometimes. One of the things that makes him so great.

"Clue," I pronounce as I stand. "But only if I get to be Colonel Mustard."

"Miss Scarlett!" Annie calls, jumping to her feet. "Mom, Dad, you guys hang out. We'll finish up in the kitchen."

I nearly argue with her, just for the sake of teasing my sister, but after the easy way our parents took our conversation, I figure cleaning up the lunch remains is the least we can do.

"Yeah, wait here," I tell them. "We might even come back with hot cocoa."

"With marshmallows!" Dad instructs as Annie and I head for the kitchen.

"Don't press your luck!" I call back, even though all of us know Dad will get his wish.

Mostly because the rest of us will want marshmallows, too.

In the kitchen, Annie and I look at each other for a second before we dissolve into relieved giggles. I plant one hand on the counter and cover my eyes with the other, the release of tension leaving me drained.

"Damn." Annie leans against the counter next to me. "I am so freaking glad that's over."

"You and me both." I get a hold of myself and, on impulse, wrap one arm around her shoulders to give her a quick squeeze. "Thanks, sis."

I know she's feeling the same way I do when she slides her

arm around my waist to return the hug. "Right back atcha."

· · ·

Later that night, after a marathon Clue tournament during which Annie wiped the floor with the rest of us, I've just changed and climbed into bed when there's a knock at the bathroom door. "Come in."

Annie pokes her head in. "That went scarily well."

I shake my head. "I'm surprised, after the way you blurted it out like that."

She sticks her tongue out as she comes over to perch on the edge of the bed. "I decided to go with the 'rip off the bandage' method."

"Usually the best way." I pick up my phone and flip it from one hand to the other. "Wish it was always that easy."

Annie shrugs. "Some things are worth a little trouble."

I give her a halfhearted glare. "Since when are you all philosophical about this?"

"Must've been that philosophy class I had to take."

"You hated that class."

She grimaces. "Of course I did. It was all either pseudobabble or simple common sense. And people get doctorates in that stuff?"

Now *that* sounds like my sister. "Stick with numbers," I advise, unnecessarily. "Numbers don't argue back."

Annie snorts. "You've never tried to find a one-character bug in a thousand lines of code."

I shudder. "And I hope I never have to."

Annie smiles but then flops back across the mattress and stares at the ceiling. "Do you think life ever gets any easier?"

"I think it gets harder," I admit. "I mean, some things get easier, sure. Other things pop up in their places." I lean back against my pillows. "Everybody's got something going on we don't know about."

Annie tips her head back to look at me upside down. "What do you think Mom and Dad have going on?"

"Worrying about us, if nothing else." I give a half smile. "And we didn't make things any easier on that front tonight."

"Ugh." Annie pushes back up and then slumps halfway off the side of the bed, arms hanging like a rag doll's. "Couldn't life slow down for once?"

"Not likely." I poke her side with my big toe. "Now get outta here. You know Dad's gonna be in here bright and early to wake us up tomorrow."

Annie snorts as she stands. "Some things never change."

She waves and heads back through the bathroom toward her room, hitting my overhead light switch and pulling the door closed behind her on the way. I lie there in the lamplight, staring up at the ceiling like she had. Off to one side, a stray glowing spot shows where we'd missed a spot removing the old set of glow-in-the-dark stars from my childhood. I kind of wished we'd kept them, though my sixteen-year-old self would scoff at that.

My sixteen-year-old self could suck it. I turn off the lamp and close my eyes, picturing the shapes of the constellations I'd made, with Dad's help, when I was seven years old. There was a crooked Big Dipper, a wonky Orion, and a wide *W* that Dad had told me was Cassiopeia, though I ended up calling it "Cassie" for short. And then we scattered the rest of the stars around at random to symbolize the Milky Way.

I laugh as I remember my determination back then to be an astronaut. That lasted a year or two, until I started doing well enough in my gymnastics classes to decide *that* was what I wanted to be when I grew up. I've mostly stuck with it, though my goals have shifted over the years.

Sometimes I miss that wide-eyed kid—the little boy who wanted nothing more out of life than to read with his mom and learn to ride a bicycle and tease his twin sister and maybe someday get the chance to chase after the stars.

I sigh into the darkness. The stars are still out there, but they're doing fine on their own. My goals have shifted closer to home. School, gymnastics, family, friends...and Darryn. Always Darryn.

I pick up my phone again and pull up our text message thread. I don't know how to start, so I dive right in.

I came out to my parents tonight.

The response takes only minutes. *Wow, go you. How'd that go?*

I blow out a breath. *It went great, actually. Easier than I thought it would.*

I'm glad, Darryn replies. *I know that's got to be a relief.*

Yeah. Despite my best efforts, my eyes are falling shut. *I must've been more tense about it than I realized, because now all I want to do is sleep.*

Then sleep. I'd sing you a lullaby, but that'd just be painful for everyone.

I smile at my phone. *See you tomorrow?*

See you tomorrow. Sleep well.

I set down my phone, roll onto my side, and close my eyes, reaching for a mental image of Darryn smiling to take me to sleep.

Works like a charm.

Chapter Twelve

Late Saturday afternoon, I walk through drizzling rain from the car to the Kanekos' front porch, my backpack over one shoulder. The weather's been nasty all day, wet and chilly, which made our family tradition of going to get a Christmas tree that morning a freezingly fun time. I'd had to change clothes right down to my underwear after we got home.

Darryn's mom must have been watching for me, because the door opens as I hit the top step. She gives me a soft, warm look and a small but genuine smile.

"Hello, Grant." Her speech is still measured and formal, but her manner is open and welcoming, and I find myself responding with my own heartfelt smile, not the polite one I had in reserve.

"Hi, Mrs. Kaneko."

"Please, come in." Mrs. Kaneko steps back to allow me inside. The room is warm and dry, and I relax into the feeling immediately.

"I'm in here, Grant."

I give Mrs. Kaneko a nod and head toward the living room,

following the sound of Darryn's voice. I find him nestled into one end of the long leather sofa with his biology book and a notebook and pen on the coffee table in front of him.

I stop in my tracks and drink in the sight of him—whole, smiling, and right in front of me for the first time in months. My chest constricts, and I can't hold back a grin as I move toward him. As I lower my backpack to the floor and myself onto the opposite end of the couch, I notice that his injured wrist rests on a pillow in his lap, but he's not wearing a sling. His gaze follows mine, and I lift an eyebrow in silent question.

"I've gotten the okay to go a few hours at a time without the sling," he tells me. "No heavy lifting and no reaching." He shrugs the uninjured side only. "It's a little sore. Feels good not to have that thing pinning me down."

"I bet." I glance at his wrist before returning my attention to his handsome face. "How's the healing?"

"Too slow. I mean," he adds quickly, "it's fine as far as healing goes. It's still taking for-freaking-ever." He runs the fingers of his free hand along the edge of the splint. "At least I get this thing off on Monday."

"Really?" I pull a throw pillow into my lap and wrap an arm around it, in part to give me something to do with my hands to keep me from reaching out to touch him. "I figured it would be longer than that."

"Oh, I won't be free." He lifts his arm and then lays it back down. "I'll have a smaller splint for a few weeks, depending on how things go, and probably a brace for support after that. Once this is off, I can start physical therapy on my wrist, at least."

I bite back the next question I want to ask, not wanting to bring up gymnastics. He reads my mind anyway.

"Six weeks of physical therapy," he tells me, "then a strength test. If I pass, I can start light weights. Six weeks after that, they *might* let me start practice again. With a lot of limitations even then."

Quick mental math tells me that's at least mid-March. Which means…

"No competition this year," Darryn confirms my silent calculations. He shrugs his healthy shoulder again. "It sucks, but not really anything anyone can do about it."

I nod. "Rushing it would just mean reinjury."

We've both been injured before. Many times over, to be honest. Most gymnasts at the college and elite levels have practiced and competed hurt for at least part of their careers. But a light strain or a blister is a far cry from a serious sprain *plus* a dislocated shoulder.

Our joints take enough abuse as it is. Overdoing it during recovery from Darryn's injuries would risk permanent injury—the kind that could have repercussions outside the gym.

"Anyway." Darryn leans forward to snag his notebook. "That's what I have to look forward to. Right now, I need to get up to speed on bio. Won't do me any good to get back to tumbling form if I don't have the grades to compete." He snorts out a short laugh. "At least I'm right-handed."

I bend down to dig my textbook and notebook out of my backpack. "Your grades will be fine," I reassure him. "And even if they weren't, you know the school's not going to dock you after what Rich—I mean, after what happened."

Darryn freezes, staring at me. "I need to tell you something."

My heart sinks. "I don't like the sound of that."

Darryn's gaze flits away from mine. "I almost called the school to ask them to drop the reports against Rich."

I sink back against the cushions. "Darryn."

He holds up his uninjured hand. "I know, I know. Dad talked me out of it. And he was right." He lets the hand fall onto the sofa cushion. "I just want it to be *over*, you know? I'm tired of being in limbo. My wrist is healing, my shoulder's a million times better, but even after I'm back to one hundred percent and out on the mats, he's still going to be hanging over my head."

I wish I could slide over and wrap my arms around him. My body aches for it, but I hold myself back. "I know it has to suck," I say instead, feeling wholly inadequate.

"Yeah." He picks at a loose thread on the cushion. "And intellectually, I know it's the right thing to do. To make him face up to what he did and to get closure or whatever for me. But I…"

"Want it to be over," I finish. That's a sentiment I share with my whole heart. "I know this is easier said than done, but try not to think about it? You have schoolwork to do and physical therapy coming up, plus there's the holidays and all that. You have plenty to keep you distracted. Don't worry about what's happening with him unless you have to."

A small smile tips up the corners of Darryn's mouth, and he looks up at me from under his lashes. "You planning to help keep me distracted?"

Lust slams into me like a rocket, and it's all I can do to hold back a gasp. *Holy shit.* With everything else that's been going on, keeping my attraction to Darryn internal and not external has become second nature. Apparently one little flirtatious comment is enough to blow the lid right off.

I breathe through it until I can speak. "I'll do what I can," I manage. "How about we start with biology? Notes, I mean," I scramble to add as the smile on his face grows into a knowing grin. "Let's go over my notes."

Darryn lets me squirm for another few moments before he picks up his notebook and pen. "All right, catch me up," he says. "What do I need to know from chapter ten?"

• • •

We fall into the studying routine easily, which is great, because it gives me a chance to recover from Darryn's moment of suggestiveness and prepare myself in case he does it again. A part of me is dancing with joy, both that he's recovered enough from The Asshole to feel like flirting and that he still sees me as a potential target of his affection. Okay, I'm assuming on that last part, but considering he never pulled anything quite that overt during the first year we knew each other, that's gotta mean something, right?

We spend the next two hours going over my biology notes—I brought photocopies so he wouldn't have to rewrite anything—and referring back to the textbook when needed. By the time we're done, Darryn's copies are covered with highlights and notes where my handwriting had gotten illegible. He's filled a page and a half in his notebook, too. When he finally leans back and lets his pen drop, he smiles.

"I think that's it," he says. "I need to take two quizzes to cover those chapters by tomorrow night. Then I'll be caught up. Thank you." His tone is earnest, and he's looking at me in such an open and honest way, I find myself holding my breath. "I never could've gotten this done that fast without your help."

My face heats, and I let out a shaky exhale. "It's not a big deal. I don't mind helping."

"Yeah, I know." He leans forward to slide his notebook onto the coffee table. "I still appreciate it. So just say you're welcome and get over it."

I roll my eyes. "You're welcome and get over it."

I stick out my tongue, and even though I know it's childish, I don't care because Darryn laughs. I decide that's my goal for every time we get together from now on, to make Darryn laugh. If that means acting silly, so be it.

A door closes down the hall and footsteps head in our direction. I clap a hand over my mouth and widen my eyes, and Darryn laughs again, just as his dad comes around the corner and into the room.

"Now, what's all this?" He crosses his arms over his chest and surveys us with what's supposed to be suspicion, but the amusement in his eyes gives him away. "I thought you two were supposed to be studying, not acting the fool."

"We've decided to change schools, Dad," Darryn says, shooting me a wink. "We're dropping out of U of A and transferring to clown college. What do you think?"

Mr. Kaneko plants both hands on his hips and lifts one eyebrow. "I think you're both naturals. I'll spring for your first bottle of seltzer."

Darryn cracks up then and we all laugh, Mr. Kaneko's more subdued but no less amused. He starts to lower himself into his recliner when a voice from the kitchen stops him.

"Ken, could you come empty the trash? It's overflowing, and I'm in the middle of dinner."

Mr. Kaneko lets out a fake, put-upon sigh. "A husband's work is never done." He winks again. "Even when there's two husbands. Keep that in mind for your future, boys."

I stare, open-mouthed, as he crosses the room and disappears into the kitchen. Darryn looks as surprised as me, but the expression quickly gives way to embarrassment. "Sorry about that," he mutters. "I had no idea he would even *think* something like that, much less *say* it."

I try to shrug it off, but my heated ears and neck have got to be giving me away. "Hey, at least he's okay with… everything," I finish lamely. "A lot of people aren't so lucky."

Darryn's expression softens. "Yeah." He glances back toward the kitchen. "They've been awesome through all this. I…I didn't…" He stops and takes a breath. "I hadn't told them. I mean"—he bites his lip—"about me. Not until we were at the hospital."

I can't imagine how that conversation went. At least when I told my parents, I had Annie there as backup. "I wasn't sure. When I saw them at the hospital, I didn't say anything because I didn't want to out you if you hadn't…you know."

"Yeah." Darryn blows out a shaky breath. "Bad enough that their son was hurt. They found out that it was his boyfriend who did it, and they didn't even know I was dating *anyone*, much less a guy."

My heart constricts as I think of him having to come out to his parents while in serious pain, from an emergency room bed. It'd been hard enough doing it from the comfort of my living room sofa.

"I'm sorry." It's all I can think of to say. "I'm sorry you had to go through that. *All* of that. I'm sorry I screwed things up. I'm sorry I didn't get into our room faster that night. I'm sorry—"

I don't know how Darryn moves that fast with his injuries. Between one word and the next, he's across the sofa, laying his uninjured hand over my mouth. I suck in a breath and my gaze snaps to his, finding his shining brown eyes full of warmth and humor.

"Shut up." The words are soft and affectionate. "It's not your fault. None of it. I know the past few months have been hard for you, too. Not in the same way," he continues when I try to interrupt, "but I know it's been painful."

He sits back and slides his hand down until his fingertips are brushing my lips, which are suddenly incredibly sensitive. "I wish I could say it's all over and everything's fine now." He lets his hand fall away and wraps it around mine where it sits on my thigh. "It's not fine. Not yet. But I promise you"—he squeezes my hand—"it will be."

His vow sinks into my bones, soothing every ache, a balm to my soul. I bring my other hand up to cover his. "It will," I tell him. "We're going to be just fine."

He smiles, and I feel as if I could live in that moment forever.

Chapter Thirteen

"Clark! You're up!"

It's late Tuesday afternoon, halfway into our first practice since Thanksgiving break, and I'm standing at the end of the vault runway, my feet and hands dusted with chalk. I nod to acknowledge Coach Everson's direction and move into position a couple of feet up from the end of the runway. Vault has never been my best apparatus, though I'm glad to be using a modern vaulting table, which is four feet wide by three feet deep, not the long, narrow horse from years ago. By the time I was old enough to attempt the vault, the old version had been relegated to the scrap heap of history.

I fix my gaze on a much more reasonable target—the springboard that sits in front of the vault table. I lift one arm to signal my intent to start my run, take a deep breath, tip up onto my toes, and then take off down the run.

Officially, it's just over eighty feet from the end of the runway to the front edge of the vault. In practice, it's a skip, a hop, fourteen running steps, and one big leap onto the springboard. I hit the sweet spot with both feet and bounce into the air, making a half turn before hitting the vault with both hands, and push back off, bringing my arms in tight to make another one and a half turns in the air. I hit the mat solidly and, with a little effort, manage to stay there—sticking the landing.

I pump one fist in celebration but head directly toward Coach Everson for correction. It felt good, but *good* isn't *perfect*. There's always something more to be done.

Coach gives me a pat on the shoulder and a nod in recognition of my work, then launches into his commentary. It's mostly everything I've heard before—punch up harder for more height, tighten up the rotation—but before he finishes, there's a commotion off to the side, people chattering and cheering.

I turn to see Darryn standing a few feet inside the gymnasium door.

My heart flips over in my chest, and a grin breaks across my face. I jog in his direction, never mind that I've left Coach in mid-instruction. I'll run laps for that one later, I'm sure. I don't even care.

I pull up to a stop in front of Darryn, still smiling.

"Hi." It's all I can think of to say.

He almost smiles. "Hi."

The rest of the team joins us before we can get past that awkward first moment. There are smiles and laughter and (gentle) slaps on the back, until finally Coach Everson intervenes.

"All right, guys, let's give him room to breathe." He wraps an arm around Darryn's shoulders. "Come on over. We'll get you a front-row seat." He tosses a quick glance at the rest of us. "Everybody else, get back to work."

Everyone else scatters, but I can't. I follow Darryn and Coach over to the front row of seats nearest the floor exercise mat and hover—there's no other word for it—while Darryn sits.

"Glad to have you back, Kaneko," Coach tells him. He turns my way. "I said back to work, Clark. You can schmooze later."

I bite back a retort and nod instead. "Yes, Coach." With one last, lingering look at Darryn, I turn and jog back over to the vault. I have at least two more runs to complete before we're done, and I want to get them out of the way so I can get back to Darryn.

The next half hour gives me a crash course in compartmentalizing. It takes all my concentration to push aside the knowledge that Darryn is across the room—that Darryn is watching, probably—and zero in on the vault. I might get away with my thoughts drifting on another apparatus, but the vault is unique. The punishment for losing focus here can be pretty severe.

I make my required two more runs, plus a third after I fumble the landing on the second. Coach Everson gives me some final instruction and then slaps me on the shoulder. "All right, go. I know you're dying to talk to him."

I flash a grin and head back across the floor. Darryn smiles as I approach and pats the bench next to him with the tips of the fingers on his left hand. That arm is still wrapped with a brace that stretches almost up to the elbow, and his right arm's still in a sling. I take the seat next to him and nod at the latter.

"How's it hangin'?"

He follows my gaze and snorts out a laugh. "I keep telling my physical therapist it's fine, it doesn't hurt. She keeps making me wear the thing anyway. I'm hoping I'll get to leave it behind before much longer."

Heath comes over then, and for the next twenty minutes, Darryn chats with various teammates as they visit to check in with him. Much as I'd prefer to have him to myself, at least I get to sit next to him.

Finally, Coach Sato comes over. "Clark, you should probably get a shower before the custodial staff comes in."

I glance around and realize the three of us are the only ones left in the gym. Darryn elbows me in the side.

"Yeah, you're starting to stink the place up. Get going."

I shove him back—gently—and do as I'm told. Coach Sato takes my seat, leaving me to wonder what they discuss while I'm gone.

I'm not gone long. It's one of the fastest showers I've ever taken after practice, and it's maybe ten minutes before I'm dressed and back out on the floor. Darryn and Coach are still talking, but they stop and stand as I approach.

Coach Sato claps Darryn on his good shoulder. "Good to see you, Kaneko. Keep up that PT. We want you back out on the mats as soon as possible."

Darryn nods. "On it, Coach."

Coach Sato gives me a nod and then heads off toward the locker rooms. I turn back to Darryn. "So." I hike my backpack higher on my shoulder. "Do you have to head back home, or can you hang around a while?"

Darryn crooks up one corner of his mouth. "Dad dropped me off. He and Mom were going out to dinner with friends, and they'll pick me up on the way back home. I've *so* been missing the dining hall the past few weeks."

I could cut that sarcasm with a machete. "I'm sure home cooking is getting to be a real drag," I send back. "How about pizza at Charlie's? Pretty sure the car's available."

"Perfect."

Darryn grins, and we head toward the door without another word. In sync, like we always have been.

I try not to read too much into that, but Darryn is by my side again, and my heart is soaring.

• • •

Twenty minutes later, we're settled into a booth at the pizza parlor where we usually order for delivery. It's not crowded, not unusual for a Tuesday, though it's packed on weekend nights. Probably because they offer a 10 percent discount on dine-in orders with student ID, as the sign in the window proudly proclaims.

I reach for the laminated menus in the small rack against the wall, but as I hand one to Darryn, he glances around. "Don't they have a buffet during the week?"

I'm sitting with my back to the dining room, but I look over my shoulder and don't see one set up. "Maybe Wednesdays?"

Darryn nods. "Yeah, I think it might've been a Wednesday the last time we were in. It's been a while."

"Yeah." I think for a second. "Maybe the second week of classes?"

"Something like that." Darryn skims the menu, though after ordering from here a couple of times a month for nearly a year and a half, we likely have it memorized. I follow his lead, though, and settle on something a little different— personal veggie pizza with banana peppers. I set my menu down just as a server arrives.

We place our orders and sit back to wait for our drinks and food. Darryn fiddles with the unnecessary flatware on the table so long that I'm tempted to slap my hand down over his. It's obvious that he's working through something, though. I give him time, and eventually he speaks up.

"I realized I owe you an apology."

I freeze at Darryn's words. "What could you possibly—"

"You tried to tell me," he continues, as if I hadn't interrupted. "You told me what Annie and Mo said about how Rich was acting, and I blew you off. No matter what was going on between us, I shouldn't have done that. I'm sorry."

He still has his focus completely on the knife, fork, and spoon lying on the scuffed wooden tabletop, though he's stopped shifting them around. He's curled his hands together, and if he didn't still have a brace covering one of them, I'd imagine he'd be wringing them.

My heart twists to see him so obviously hurting, and I don't stop myself from reaching out this time. I lay one of my hands over his. "You don't owe me anything," I tell him. "You cared about him. You didn't want to think he'd do anything like…" I don't need to finish that statement. "It's not your fault."

A shudder runs through him. "I feel like an idiot," he whispers.

My stomach plummets. "You aren't," I reassure him as I squeeze his hands gently. "You're a good guy who expects other people to be good, too. He took advantage of that. And that's on him, not you. Never you."

We sit in silence for a few minutes, until Darryn finally takes a long, stuttering breath and blows it out. He flips over his good hand and squeezes mine.

"I'm trying to believe that," he says, his voice stronger. "Maybe eventually I will."

He finally looks up then, his eyes wet but the tears unshed, and he gives a small, shaky smile.

"Well." I return the smile with a tiny one of my own. "If you ever need reminding, let me know."

"I will." He squeezes my hand one more time before he lets go and leans back in his seat. "Tell me about this thing with you and Kenny Washington."

I blink at the sudden shift in his attitude, but I don't ask. I just go with it.

"You know I want to coach eventually, right? Well, one day I saw Kenny working on the floor …"

• • •

With finals over and four full weeks of winter break freedom ahead of us, Annie and I are back home, loads of dirty laundry in tow. Mom always says she's going to make us do it ourselves, but somehow that never happens. She does, however, make us sort it, so that's what we're doing when Annie finally broaches the subject I'd been expecting.

"How are things going with Darryn?"

I let out a breath and toss another towel into the appropriate bin. "Better," I tell her. "We're actually talking about things now, which is an improvement over letting it all stew."

"Funny how that works."

I snort. "Yeah, yeah. Communication, what a concept!"

Annie shoots me a grin. "Do you have plans to see each other over the holidays?"

I shrug a shoulder. "Don't know yet. I don't know what his family plans are. But I hope so."

"What did you get him for Christmas?"

My brain freezes. "*Dammit.*"

Annie laughs at me as I grab for my phone to start searching for ideas. I'm only a few words into a Google search when my phone buzzes and it's a text from Darryn. *Have you headed home yet?*

I smile as I type out a response. *Yep. Sorting laundry now. Four whole weeks of freedom ahead of me!*

Must be nice, he replies. *I still have to finish up in bio. The online class runs a few days longer.*

Ugh. Need any help studying?

Thanks, I should be okay.

"Oh, I know that look."

I jerk my head up to see Annie smirking at me. My face heats, but the smile doesn't leave my face.

"Yeah, yeah." I shove her shoulder. "I'll make you a deal.

I'll clean up after dinner if you'll finish sorting this stuff for me?"

Annie snorts. "As long as I don't have to deal with dirty underwear, you've got a deal." She nods at my phone as it buzzes again. "Go talk to your boy."

"Yes, ma'am." I sketch a mock salute and head for my bedroom, reading his latest message as I go. *Are you busy for New Year's?*

Like it matters. If Darryn wants us to spend New Year's together, I will be there with bells on.

I push my bedroom door shut and perch on the edge of my bead before I reply. *No real plans. Having a party?*

No party. Just me and my parents. We do some traditional Japanese stuff that's kinda cool. You're welcome to come if you want.

Oh, I *want,* but I tamp down my over-eagerness. *Sure. Sounds like fun. What time?*

Eight is good. We eat dinner late because we stay up late. Mom makes sushi.

Score! Then I'll be there at eight. Let me know if I can bring anything.

Just yourself, comes the reply. *That's all I need.*

I fall back onto the bed, unable to stop smiling.

• • •

Darryn's words settle deep in my heart, carrying me through the week until I can see him again. Christmas comes and goes like it usually does—lots of food, lots of gifts, lots of family time. I try to soak it all in. Maybe it's being out to my parents, maybe it's everything that's gone on with Darryn, but the holidays feel fragile this year. Like a bubble stretched tight, just before it pops.

Everyone's fine with me going to Darryn's for New

Year's. Annie's not much for partying anyway, and Mom and Dad usually stay home and have their own champagne toast.

"Give him our best, dear," Mom says when I head out. "And drive safely!"

"Yes, ma'am," I reply, ever the dutiful son.

My left leg won't stop bouncing during the hour-long trip to the Kanekos' house—nearly twice as long as it usually takes, thanks to all the revelers heading out to celebrate. I pull into the driveway fifteen minutes later than I planned, and I've barely gotten out of the car when the front door opens and Darryn stands there in the soft glow of the porch light.

My breath catches. He's dressed casually, jeans and a T-shirt, socks on his feet. He's absolutely gorgeous, and the light in his eyes as he smiles at me carries me forward, feeling as if my feet aren't even touching the ground.

I swallow and throw one hand up in a wave as I walk toward him, trying to keep a mantra of *just friends* running through my head.

It doesn't work all that well, but I'm trying.

Three hours later, I'm stuffed full after Mrs. Kaneko's noodles—Darryn's dad had explained that toshi-koshi soba were traditional on New Year's Eve, symbolizing long life—and the green tea ice cream we had for dessert. We'd even done a gift exchange, Darryn's parents offering me a traditional gift of a small decorated envelope filled with yen, which they tell me are called otoshidama. Before I can feel bad about not bringing them a gift, Darryn laughs and says the gifts are traditionally for children, and the money inside adds up to only a few US dollars. "Think of it as a party favor," he suggests, so I smile and thank his parents.

Darryn's face lit up when he opened the new insulated water bottle I'd picked out for him—it was designed to be easy to use one-handed. That went nicely with the T-shirt he gave me, which pictured a cartoon brain tumbling on a gym mat with the caption "Mental Gymnastics." Nothing awkward or too much, to my great relief.

Now, with midnight fast approaching, I'm settled on the sofa opposite Darryn, his parents in their chairs off to one side, as one of the midnight countdown shows flashes across the television in front of us. None of us is paying it much attention, though. We're much too involved in what has to be the most cutthroat game of Mahjong in history. Though if all Japanese women play the way Mrs. Kaneko does, our version could be relatively tame.

Either way, the rest of us are losing. Badly. I have an excuse, considering I'd never played Mahjong in any form except the basic computerized version before tonight. But Darryn and his dad aren't faring any better than I am.

I've lost track of what time it is when Mrs. Kaneko beats us, again, and Mr. Kaneko throws in the towel—or the tiles. "All right, that's all the fun I can handle for one night." He slaps his hands onto his thighs and then pushes to his feet. "Come along, my dear. Let's leave the boys to it."

I blink up at him. "Not waiting until midnight?"

He winks. "We prefer to celebrate on our own."

My cheeks heat, but he laughs. "We'll have more celebration tomorrow. Ozoni for breakfast. Grilled mochi and vegetable soup, basically," he explains for my benefit. "We pull out all the Japanese stops on New Year's Day."

"Grant, you're welcome to stay if you like." Mrs. Kaneko offers a small smile and nods toward the hall. "The guest room's made up."

I'm surprised but return her smile. "I'll probably head home pretty soon after midnight, but thank you for the offer."

She nods again. "Good night, boys."

She heads down the hall, and Mr. Kaneko gives us a smile and a wink. "Don't get too crazy out here."

Darryn laughs. "We'll keep it down. See you in the

morning."

His dad disappears down the hall, and then it's just us, the silent Times Square celebration on the TV, and the glasses of sparkling grape juice on the coffee table in front of us. I reach for mine and take a sip, but as I set it back down, Darryn slides from his chair.

"C'mon," he says. "It's almost midnight. Let's go watch the neighbors set off fireworks."

I lift an eyebrow but follow him onto the front porch. Darryn sits on the porch swing at one end and pats the seat next to him.

"Best view in town, promise."

He smiles, and there's nothing on earth that could make me say no.

I settle onto the swing, leaving as much space between us as I can without shoving myself up against the arm. I don't want to crowd him, but I don't want to look like I don't want to be anywhere near him. If I let myself do what I really want, I'd slide right up to his side and wrap my arm around his shoulders to keep him as close as possible.

I mentally shake off the image and give the swing a tiny push. "Is this how you usually spend New Year's Eve?" I ask. "Swingin' on the porch, watchin' the neighbors blow shit up?"

Darryn chuckles. "Sometimes." He pushes one foot against the floor to keep the swing going. "Some years it's too cold. Sometimes I don't want to stay up. Most years, though, yeah. We moved here when I was ten, and probably six or seven times I've spent midnight on the porch."

I tilt my head up at a whistling sound, and sure enough, a few seconds later a small multicolor burst lights the air a few houses down the street. "I guess the show's gotten better since they legalized fireworks?"

"A little, yeah. They had some pretty fancy stuff even ten years ago."

We fall silent as a few more fireworks flash in the air and cheers go up in response. The pungent smell and smoke drift our way, but there's enough of a breeze to keep it from hanging around long enough to irritate.

The silence between us isn't uncomfortable, but I'm trying to come up with something to break it when the partiers down the street start counting. "Ten! Nine! Eight!"

I don't know how accurate their count is, but I turn my head toward Darryn anyway, only to find him much closer than he'd been minutes before. He's smiling softly and his gaze captures me, drawing me in like a moth to a flame. My heart pounds, a hot flush runs over my skin, and all concepts of *just a friend* evaporate from my mind.

The revelers cheer as their countdown ends, and for that moment, everything in the world is right.

"Happy New Year," I whisper.

"Happy New Year." Darryn's smile slips and his gaze flicks down to my lips. I catch my breath, but before I can do anything, he leans forward to kiss me.

It's a brief thing, a press and slow retreat, and I don't have a chance to kiss him back. His hand wraps around mine and he smiles again.

"I'm not ready yet," he says, his voice still soft, though the words echo through my head as if he'd shouted. "But I trust you not to hurt me. And I'll get there. I promise."

I flip my hand over to squeeze his fingers with mine. "I'll be waiting," I murmur back. "I promise."

Darryn inches closer and leans his head on my shoulder, and I swallow back a million words I want to say. We've said the things that matter most.

Instead, I settle in to watch the rest of the neighbors' fireworks show, no longer feeling the chill in the air. All the warmth I need, I have right here with Darryn by my side, his hand held securely in mine.

Chapter Fourteen

"That's the last of it."

Mr. Kaneko sets two bags on the foot of Darryn's bed and gives me a smile. "Thank you for all your help, Grant. I don't know if we could have gotten everything upstairs on our own."

I shrug. "It's no problem. I'm glad to have Darryn back."

Darryn perches on the edge of his bed. "Man. I didn't realize how out of shape I am. It's not like I even carried anything." Still on orders for no heavy lifting, he'd been relegated to nothing more than his laptop bag and his brand-new rolling backpack, a Christmas gift from his parents.

"Slacker." I grin as he makes a face at me, knowing that without his dad there, he'd probably have flipped me off instead.

"All right." Mr. Kaneko smiles. "I'll leave you boys to it." He steps over to clap Darryn on his good shoulder. "We'll see you Friday."

"Thanks, Dad." Darryn stands and pulls his father into a hug. I don't remember ever seeing him do that before. They've always seemed to have a good relationship, but they seem closer now. I'm dying to ask for details, but that's not exactly how I want to lead off our first day back as roommates.

They separate, and then Mr. Kaneko turns to me, hand out to shake. "Grant."

I take his hand. "Mr. Kaneko."

He smiles. "Call me Ken, son."

Before I can recover from the surprise, he's closing the door behind him. I turn to Darryn, who looks half a second away from a laugh. "Did that just happen?"

"Congrats," Darryn says. "You're the first of my friends to ever get first-name basis from my dad."

I'm still stunned but I try to shake it off. "Okay, then." I frown. "What's that about Friday?"

"Oh." Darryn waves toward the brace on his wrist. "We got my physical therapy sessions scheduled for late Friday afternoons. Since it's up near the house, Mom's going to pick me up after class, and I'll spend the night with them and come back Saturday."

"I guess that makes sense." I put my hands on my hips and turn to look at the mess surrounding us. "And I guess we should deal with all this, too."

Darryn groans but reaches for one of the bags on his bed. "Might as well get it over with."

Two hours later, we've managed to get most of our stuff put away, and we're headed to the dining hall. I'd been worried that things might be awkward between us, especially after the New Year's kiss neither of us has brought up again, but we've slotted right back into being friends and roommates. When we get to the food line, Darryn teases me about my addiction to sweet tea, and I respond by threatening to take away his ketchup. We find a seat near the windows, and we're settling in when Annie and Mo walk through the door.

Mo nudges Annie, and they wave as they head to the line.

I glance at Darryn. "Do you mind if Annie and Mo join us?"

Darryn freezes for a split second, but then relaxes and shrugs his good shoulder. "Sure. I mean, I don't really know Mo, but she seems nice."

"Yeah. I just…" I'm not sure how to approach the subject.

Darryn saves me the trouble.

"I appreciate that they tried to help," he says, keeping his voice low. "I just don't want to talk about all that right now."

I nod and give a tiny smile. "Shouldn't be a problem. We can focus on whining about our classes instead."

Annie and Mo join us a few minutes later. "Hello, boys," Mo says as she swings into a seat next to Darryn. "Are we ready to get back to the grind?"

I exchange a glance with Annie, whose lifted eyebrow tells me she and Mo had an exchange much like the one Darryn and I just had. "Ready to start taking classes in my major," I say. "I finally got into the kinesiology intro this semester."

"Oh, me too!" Mo grins. "Are you in the Monday-Wednesday-Friday session?"

"Yep." I lift my tea in a mock toast. "See you then, I guess!"

Mo turns to Darryn. "How about you? Anything interesting?"

Darryn shrugs. "Yeah, I have intro to nutrition. The incomplete in chemistry threw things off, though."

He freezes then, probably realizing he brought up the very subject he wanted to avoid, but Mo glides right over it like it's no big deal. "Ugh, right? I guess it's better than having to take the whole class over. Still probably made a mess of your schedule."

"Yeah." Darryn relaxes minutely. "I might make it up over the summer. Or take something else to free up a spot for next fall." He shrugs again. "We'll get it worked out one way or another."

I move on to Annie. "How about you? Still taking way too many hours?"

Annie rolls her eyes. "Eighteen hours is not 'too many.' Just because you wimp out and only take fifteen…"

"The required course load," I shoot back. "And with two hours of practice four days a week, there's no time for more than that."

She knows all of that, of course. It's standard sibling stuff.

Mo giggles at us. "I'm in the same boat as Grant," she tells Annie. "I'm on the court or in the gym two or three hours a day. Really cuts into the studying time, but the scholarship requires it."

Annie sighs. "I wish my scholarship would pay for my private room. I need to drum up some more business if I want to keep it next year."

"We'll help you out," Mo assures her. "There's always someone with some kind of tech problem. Right, Grant?"

"Right." I shoot my best grin at Annie. "As long as I still get the twin discount."

Annie tosses a pea at me. "Watch it, or I'll charge you double."

Darryn's low chuckle draws my attention back to him. "Life keeps chugging along, doesn't it?" He sounds philosophical, as if he'd put a lot of thought into what he's saying. "No matter what happens. All the ups and downs. Life goes on."

I catch and hold his gaze, and he gives me a private smile. Yeah, life goes on. And I'm incredibly glad I've got Darryn here to share it with.

• • •

The whirlwind of the first days of classes catches up with

us, and it's not until Wednesday after practice that we get a chance to breathe. Coach let us out a little bit early, so Darryn and I are back in our room, the windows and door open to take advantage of a rare warm January day and air things out. Voices and music filter in through both openings, not loud enough to be distracting.

We're both reading, me sitting on my bed and Darryn at his desk, when there's a knock from the doorway. I look over to see Pace grinning at us.

"Hi, guys! Mind if I come in?"

"Sure." Darryn answers before me, though he sounds puzzled. And I realize he probably doesn't know about Pace and me working out together back in the fall. Not that it became any big thing, but it's something that I usually would've brought up.

Pace drops into my empty desk chair. "How're you doing? If you don't mind me asking, I mean."

Darryn gives him a small smile. "Getting there. Healing. Doing physical therapy."

"Great!" Pace's smile never dims. "We should work out together sometime."

Darryn shoots me a questioning look. "I can't really—"

"You can still do legs stuff, right? Maybe some cardio? I can spot for you if you need me to."

Something about the eager look on his face tells me why he's pushing on this. I think he just wants to help. To *do something.* And offering to spot for our workouts while Darryn recovers is something he can do.

"Sure, that'd probably be great," I tell him, glancing at Darryn to try to gauge his reaction. He still looks puzzled, but he lets me do the talking. "We'll figure out what our schedules look like and let you know."

"Cool." Pace bounces out of his seat. "Guess I better go get some work done. First quiz in geography tomorrow and I haven't done the reading. Later!"

He's out the door and gone before either of us can answer, and all I can do is shake my head. Darryn takes one look at my face and cracks up.

"Sorry," he forces out. "You look like I feel. A little bit stunned, a little bit dizzy, and a whole lotta 'what the hell just happened?'"

I have to join in his laughter. "Par for the course with Pace, I guess." I wave a hand toward the door. "He spotted for me a couple of times last semester when you were—when you couldn't," I amend quickly. "He's kind of all over the place most of the time, but he's pretty focused in the gym." I shrug. "I don't know that much about the baseball team, but I guess everybody who's on a team has to keep up with training."

"Yeah." Darryn frowns down at his wrist. "Guess I wouldn't be much good at spotting now, either. If we work out together, all three of us, then I can do legs and cardio and you two can do the weight training part."

I lean forward to try to catch his eye. "Only if it's okay with you," I tell him. "If it bothers you, if it's too much…"

Darryn shakes his head and meets my gaze. "No, it'll be fine. I need to start facing some of this stuff head-on, y'know? It'll be a while before I'm back up to full strength, and I don't want to stay away from everything until then. I'll ease my way back in."

"That makes a lot of sense. But if you do need to leave, even in the middle of something, don't worry about it. Okay? Just go when you need to."

Darryn nods once. "Will do." He taps the open book on his desk. "Now get back to that reading, Clark."

I sketch a mock salute. "Yes, sir!"

I'm rewarded with a genuine smile, one that sends my heart soaring in my chest, and I return it before going back to my homework, warmed all the way through by the return of the Darryn I...

The Darryn I fell in love with.

I have no idea what to do with that realization. I never exactly got over Darryn—I just repressed my feelings while I tried to be his friend. I'm past that point now, but since that one tentative kiss on New Year's, Darryn hasn't shown any signs of wanting to move forward with that kind of a relationship.

I have a choice in front of me—keep repressing and pining, or find some way to cross back over that line without moving too fast for Darryn.

A balancing act harder than anything I've ever had to do in the gym.

• • •

I spend the next two weeks focusing on class, practice, and being Darryn's friend. I don't want to push him into anything he's not ready for, so I find other ways to go the extra mile. I carry his new rolling backpack outside in the morning so he doesn't have to wrestle it down the stairs. I make sure we always have a tube of the topical pain relief cream he uses when his shoulder aches. I do resist the urge to offer to rub it on for him, no matter how much I'd love to get my hands on him.

He doesn't say anything other than thanks. But the tiny smiles he sends my way completely destroy me.

By the end of the month, we've pretty much settled in to our new routine. It's a Thursday night and we're playing our homework game, Darryn on his bed and me at my desk this time. Without our usual chatter, it's more noticeable when Darryn's phone buzzes with an incoming call. It's the third time his phone has rung since we got back from dinner, and he has yet to answer one.

I keep reading, but I glance at him from the corner of my eye every few minutes. About five minutes after the last call, Darryn's phone buzzes again, and once again he swipes the call away. It's not enough for me to break the silence, but the way Darryn's curled into himself, like he's shrinking away from a threat. That does the trick.

"Darryn."

He glances up but doesn't meet my gaze. "You lose."

I set my book aside. "Yeah, I lose." I lean forward, watching his face. "Who keeps calling?"

He curls in even tighter. "It's nothing. I'm fine."

He might as well have told me. That reaction confirms exactly what I'm thinking.

"Is it Rich?"

He jerks his head up and then lets out a soft gasp and reaches for his bad shoulder—with his bad wrist, which doesn't help matters.

I wince in sympathy. "Sorry."

He shakes his head. "Not your fault. It just twinges sometimes."

"Kinda is." I don't pause long, though. Might as well plow right on through. "How long has he been calling?"

Darryn lets out a dry laugh and slumps back against the wall. "Since the day after classes started back," he admits.

I blow out a breath. "He's harassing you."

Darryn shrugs his good shoulder. "I'm not answering."

"But he keeps calling." Just as the words leave my mouth, Darryn's phone rings again, and he freezes. I jump up and cross to his side so I can see the screen. I bite back a laugh at the name displayed: RICH THE A-HOLE.

Darryn swipes to reject the call. "It's not a big deal, Grant."

I squat in front of Darryn and look up at him until he

meets my gaze. "It's bothering you," I say, keeping my voice low and soft. "I know you'll probably have to deal with him eventually, with whatever the school ends up doing. You shouldn't have to even think about him otherwise."

I slide my hand over his phone, and Darryn slowly lets go. With a few quick clicks, I block Rich's number. "There," I say, handing the phone back. "Now at least your phone won't ring when he calls."

Darryn takes the phone. "Thanks."

I step away and perch on the edge of my bed across from him. "You should report it, Darryn."

He shakes his head. "It's nothing."

"Stop saying that! It's not nothing!" I'm on my feet without realizing it, hands clenched into fists. "He's harassing you, and someone has to make him stop."

Darryn sits frozen, and as my flare of anger ebbs, I realize he's not just surprised at my outburst.

He's scared.

Shit.

I drop my hands to my sides. "Darryn, I'm—"

Before I can muster an apology, Darryn's up and grabbing his backpack. "I'm going to the library," he tells me, voice shaking. "Don't follow me."

I can't do anything but watch him go.

Shit, fuck, and damn.

Why can't I stop fucking things up?

• • •

Over the next few days, I try to let it go. I did apologize the second Darryn came back to the dorm, and he seemed to accept it, but I've been trying to avoid raising my voice or acting threatening in any kind of way. It leaves us tiptoeing around each other, but every day feels a little better.

I also don't see Darryn reject any calls, and though he's quiet and withdrawn, I suppose that's to be expected sometimes after what happened. His mind needs time to heal, same as his body.

If only my own mind would stay on track. Instead, my focus is completely shot for the rest of the week. Coach Sato gets so fed up with me on Friday that he makes me run laps at the end of practice before he releases me. I try to settle my racing thoughts over the weekend, without much luck. Darryn's gone from quiet to giving me the silent treatment, barely saying a thing and heading off to the library at the drop of a word. By Sunday night, the atmosphere in our room is so thick with words unsaid that it's hard to breathe.

Things come to a head at practice on Monday. I'm halfway through my warmup when the usual murmurs of conversation around the gym floor coalesce into a familiar name.

"Darryn!" Heath is the first across the floor, and I turn my head in time to see him clasp the man himself in a half hug. Darryn smiles, more of a grimace than anything real. A few other teammates call out to him or wave, and Coach Sato walks over to greet him and speaks to him in a low voice.

I go back to my stretches, breathing through the hollowed-out feeling in my chest. Okay. Darryn didn't tell me he was coming back to practice today. He's still working through stuff and needs space, which I've given. It doesn't hurt. Not one bit.

My inner lie detector laughs at me, and I slump to the mat, masking as a roll into another stretch. If I can't even be honest with myself, how can I be honest with Darryn?

We have *got* to get this mess worked out.

With my mind otherwise occupied, practice is a joke. I can't focus on anything, I nearly brain myself on the pommel horse when I miss a grip, and I lose it entirely on the high bar, only years of training in falling well and an ingrained sense of self-preservation saving me from a nasty fall. After that one, Coach Everson sends me to the showers early.

"Get your head together, Clark," he says. "And then see me in my office."

My stomach sinks through the floor. I don't look around as I cross toward the locker room, and inside, I slump onto the bench and stare at the wall of metal doors in front of me.

What the hell do I do now?

"Great practice."

I jerk my head up to find Darryn leaning against the wall inside the door. The overhead light flickers, leaving his face in half shadow.

"I've had worse." Doubtful, but it gives me something to say as I reach into my locker for a towel.

"I could've beaten you with my one good one arm."

A bitter laugh forces its way out of me. "Truth hurts." Though not as much as my heart.

"Grant."

Something in the tone of Darryn's voice begs for me to look his way. I refuse to give in.

"Coach wants to see me. I've gotta go."

It's a lie. Coach won't be in his office until practice ends, and Darryn knows it. He blows out a frustrated breath.

"Well, if you decide you want to talk about it—"

I blow out air in frustration and try not to glare at him. Too much. "You avoided me all weekend. Don't come in here acting like *I'm* the one who hasn't wanted to 'talk about it.'"

This time, Darryn holds his ground. "*Wanting* to and knowing where to start are two very different things." He crosses his arms over his chest. "Look. I don't want to fight with you. I want us to get past all this. That's not going to happen until we can be *honest* with each other, Grant."

My residual anger drains out of me. He's right. I know

he's right. "Okay. Well...where do we even start?"

Tension visibly drains out of his body, and he shrugs his good shoulder. "We could always try at the beginning."

A whistle sounds outside the door, signaling the end of practice, and Darryn glances over his shoulder. "I have to stop by the admin building to drop off some paperwork," he says. "I'm going back to the room after that. Can we talk then?"

I catch and hold his gaze. "I'll be there," I promise.

He smiles at me, small and private, then turns to head back out into the gym. I watch him go, hope blooming in my chest.

Maybe we can figure this out after all.

• • •

When Coach Everson makes it to his office, I'm sitting on the floor outside his door, head tipped back against the cement-block wall. Coach unlocks the door and pushes it open.

"C'mon, Clark. Up and at 'em."

I drag myself up and shuffle over to the nearest chair. Coach shuts the door, but instead of walking around to sit behind the desk, he leans against the edge of it, arms crossed over his chest. I'm afraid to look up and see the disappointment on his face.

"Your focus has been way off the past couple of practices, Grant." Understatement. "Want to tell me what's going on?"

I keep my head lowered. "Not really."

Coach blows out a breath. "Look. I've been giving you a lot of leeway here. I know you've been dealing with some personal stuff. But if it's going to keep interfering—"

"I think Rich is stalking him."

The words burst out of me like gunshots, and I wish for a second I could take them back, but when I glance up at

Coach's face, the mix of concern and anger I see there eases something inside me—probably because it matches how I feel.

"Okay." Coach moves around to sit behind the desk then, grabbing a pen and pad of paper as he goes. "Start from the beginning."

I blow out a long breath. "Rich started calling him right after classes started, apparently. I didn't find out until last week. Darryn's been rejecting the calls, but..."

I can't give voice to my fear—I'm afraid Rich might escalate, might show up at our door—but Coach seems to understand. He scribbles something on the pad of paper in front of him. "How often is he calling?"

"I don't know," I tell him. "I don't actually know if he's still calling. I got Darryn to let me block the number after he called at least four times in one day."

Coach writes down something else. "And that was when?"

"Last Thursday." I dry my damp palms on my thighs. "I've been trying to get Darryn to report it to someone, the school or at least his parents, but I can't force him. I didn't know what else to do."

Coach nails me with a look. "You don't need to do anything else. Let Coach Sato and me handle this." He holds up a hand to stop me before I can interrupt. "I know you want to help, and I know you're hoping to be where we are someday. But you aren't there yet, and he needs you to be his friend right now. Not his coach."

I know it's the truth. That doesn't mean I have to like it. "Whatever you need me to do..."

"Just be there for him." Coach eyes me for a moment. "For the record, I know there's more than friendship going on there."

I shouldn't be surprised, but a shockwave runs through me. "We aren't—"

He holds up a hand again. "I don't need details. Your personal life is yours, unless you give us a reason to be concerned." He leans back in his chair. "I know the way it's happening for Darryn is far from ideal, but coming out isn't what it used to be, and gymnastics isn't football. I doubt it'll make a difference to anyone, and I don't think there's any need for a big announcement. It's up to you what you want to do."

I wipe my sweaty palms on my pants legs. "I want to be who I am," I tell him. "And I want to be there for Darryn. Whatever that means for him."

Coach nods. "We'll support you in whatever you decide." He rocks forward, folding his hands on the desktop in front of him. "In the meantime, let *us* deal with Darryn. We'll make sure he gets any help he needs. And not only for the good of the team. Yes, we have a vested interest, but we actually do care about him as a person, not just as a gymnast."

"Yeah." I wipe my hands again. "I just want him to be okay, you know?"

"We all do. We'll get him there." Coach almost smiles. "I'd tell you not to worry, but that would be a waste of breath."

I huff out a laugh. "You're not wrong."

Coach waves a hand. "Get out of here. Go be a student for a while."

I push to my feet and give him a mock salute. "Yes, sir!"

He rolls his eyes, and I grin as I hike my backpack onto my shoulder before heading out.

• • •

When I step outside, I shiver. The sun's nearly gone, and between the sharp chill in the air and the clouds gathering overhead, I guess we're in for some cold February rain—or maybe even a few snow flurries. I hook my free arm through the other strap of my backpack so I can shove both hands into the pockets of my hoodie as I head across campus.

As I walk, I try to mentally prepare for the conversation Darryn and I need to have. I know it won't be easy, but we need to work things out. I want us to work things out. And not only because of my feelings for him. I want us to be friends again, like we were before everything happened.

And if something more is possible, then I'll count myself lucky.

Halfway back to the dorm, the first few raindrops hit my face, and I pick up my pace, hoping to avoid getting soaked. I'm almost jogging when I hit the edge of the quad, and over in front of the admin building, in the harsh yellow light of a streetlight, I see Darryn approaching from the other direction. I'm pretty attuned to him by now, of course, but even if I wasn't sure, the rolling backpack behind him would be a dead giveaway.

Screw the rain. I change my trajectory to intercept him along the way. Maybe I can convince him to head off campus for dinner—talk things out away from the scene of the crime.

Before I go more than a few yards toward him, though, a car pulls up at the curb next to him and someone jumps out and jogs around the front end. Between the darkening sky and the distance, I can't tell who it is, but when he grabs Darryn by the arm, I figure it out in a hurry and take off running.

"Hey!" My shout sounds hollow to my ears, though that could be because my pounding heartbeat drowns out everything else. "Let him go!"

In my periphery, I see heads turn in my direction, but in a flash, Rich has Darryn shoved into the car and slams the door behind him. I'm still a good fifty feet away when Rich dives into the driver's seat and takes off, the back tires fishtailing on the freshly wet pavement.

"Fuck!" I keep running until I pull to a stop next to where Darryn's backpack still sits on the sidewalk. "Shit. Shit."

I fumble for my cell phone and dial 911 while I try to catch my breath, ignoring the now-steady rainfall. Other people gather around me, and I'm sure some of them are trying to talk to me, but I turn away and plug my other ear with my free hand so I can hear when the call is answered.

"911, what's your emergency?"

"Kidnapping," I bark out. "My best friend's ex grabbed him off the sidewalk and took off with him."

Keys clatter down the line. "Where are you, sir?"

"University of Atlanta. On campus, I'm right in front of the admin building, across from the dorm quad."

"All right, sir. I'm dispatching someone now. Can you tell me exactly what happened?"

I take in as deep a breath as I can manage and give her the basics: Darryn's name, Rich's name, the fact that they split up last fall, and what I saw. "There are other people around, too." I tell her. "They'll back me up."

I glance up then, and two faces stand out. Annie and Mo have shoved their way past the gathering crowd, and they're standing right in front of me. Annie holds out a hand, and I grab it, squeezing tight. I glance at Mo.

"Go get Coach Everson," I tell her. "I just talked to him. He needs to know about this."

She's gone in a flash, and I try to focus on the dispatcher's calm voice and my grip on Annie's hand. They're the only things keeping me from breaking apart.

I hear sirens sooner than expected, though it still feels like forever. A police car turns into the campus entrance and comes to a stop nearby.

"They're here," I tell the dispatcher before ending the call. I shove my phone into my pocket, but I don't let go of Annie's hand as the officers approach.

"We have a report of a kidnapping?"

"Yeah...yes." I'm trembling, but I manage a nod. "My roommate, Darryn. He was walking back to the dorm when his ex grabbed him and took off with him."

The officer lifts an eyebrow. "You sure he didn't go with him willingly?"

I open my mouth to blast him, but Annie squeezes my hand, which pulls me back from the edge, if only an inch. "Yes, I'm sure," I bite out. "He grabbed Darryn and shoved him into the car. I saw it. And this is Darryn's backpack." I point to it, my hand shaking. "Don't you think he would've taken *that* if he'd wanted to go with him?"

The officer backs off, glancing behind him at his partner. "Bishop, collect the backpack as evidence." He pulls out a notebook. "Okay. Start at the beginning and tell me the story."

A cold sort of calm comes over me as I give the shortest summary of this entire clusterfuck that I can manage. Darryn and Rich dating, Rich turning possessive, then getting physical. Darryn's injuries and Rich's arrest. The recent repeated phone calls and texts.

I'm finishing up when running footsteps approach, and I turn to see Coach Everson arriving. "Grant," he says, placing a hand on my shoulder. "What's going on?"

And just like that, everything comes slamming back into me, and it's all I can do to keep my knees from buckling. "Rich kidnapped Darryn," I tell him. *Oh God, Rich has him, and I can't even think about what he plans to do with Darryn.* "I don't know... I called the police, but I don't..."

Coach Everson slides his hand down to my elbow, silently bracing me. "I've got you," he murmurs, and as I suck in a ragged breath, he turns his attention to the officer. "Officer..." He squints at the man's nametag. "Johnston. I'm Barry Everson, Grant and Darryn's gymnastics coach.

I know the backstory here, and if Grant here says someone took Darryn against his will, then that's what happened."

The officer nods and turns back to his partner again. "Bishop, call for backup." He faces me again. "All right. Let's start with a description of the car."

• • •

Two hours later, I'm sitting at one end of a strangely uncomfortable sofa in, of all places, the office of the university president. The man himself is out of town at the moment, but the provost set Annie and me up there to wait for word. A television behind the desk is playing a basketball game, volume set low, not that either of us is paying it any attention. Someone even brought us sandwiches and bottles of water, though I couldn't manage to eat more than a couple of bites.

I can't sit still, either. I've been up and down more times than I can count, pacing the length of the room and back until Annie forces me to sit again. It never lasts. I can't stop the images playing like scenes from a horror movie through my mind. Darryn, tied to a chair, eyes wide with terror. Bruises and cuts marring his handsome face. Rich ripping at his clothes…

That image sends bile rising in my throat. "Dammit!" I stop in the middle of the floor and dig both hands into my hair. "Why is this taking so long?"

Annie sighs. "I'm sure we'll hear something soon," she says, for what's probably the fifth time. "Rich is a garden-variety asshole, not a supervillain, and this isn't some action movie where the bad guy has a secret lair in the catacombs under the city. They'll find him, he'll go to jail, and Darryn will be fine."

I cross back to flop onto the sofa next to her. "He will. I know he will. It's the waiting that's killing me."

Annie reaches out to squeeze my trembling hand. "You'll be fine, too."

The logical part of my brain knows she's almost certainly right. The rest of me, not so much.

I stare in the direction of the television, not registering anything that's going on other than players moving around on the court. I don't even know who's playing. I can only sit and try to keep breathing.

My phone rings, and I jump forward to grab it from where it sits on the table in front of me. My heart jumps back to life in my chest when I see Darryn's picture.

I swipe to answer. "Darryn?"

"Hey." He sounds exhausted, but his voice is steady. "I called the cops. They got Rich."

"Oh, thank God." I'm on my feet and pacing again, even though my whole body is shaking. "Where are you?"

"In the back of a black and white, on my way to the hospital again." There's a hint of humor in his voice, and that more than anything else allows me to relax by an inch.

I stop pacing and turn to meet Annie's gaze. "We'll meet you there," I promise him. "Should I... Did someone call your parents?"

"The cops are doing that already," he tells me. "They're on the way, too."

The door to the hallway opens, and I spin around again as Coach Everson steps inside. Our gazes meet, and he gives a small smile.

"Darryn called in," he tells us.

"I know," I reply, pointing at the phone. "I'm on with him right now."

His smile shows the same relief I'm feeling. I glance back at Annie, and she's rolling her eyes at me, but she's smiling, too.

Relief washes over me like a blessing. "We're heading to

the hospital now," I tell all three of them.

"I'll see you there," Darryn replies.

• • •

I could've done without ever coming back to this emergency room, but considering Darryn's preexisting injuries, I'm glad he'd played it safe and let the police take him in to be checked over. I follow Coach Everson toward the desk, where he gives his name and Darryn's. The nurse says something I don't hear, and Coach turns back to me.

"They'll let his parents know we're here." He waves toward the nearby row of chairs. "Have a seat."

I do as I'm told, though I'm still so antsy that I can't keep my legs from bouncing like they're on springs. I try deep breathing. It doesn't help anything.

I won't be able to settle down until I can see for myself that Darryn is okay.

Under the white noise of the mechanical beeping, soft footsteps, and distant chatter surrounding us, I hear a low buzzing, and Coach pulls his phone out of his pocket. He taps the screen a few times and then glances my way.

"They've booked Rich. He'll probably be charged with kidnapping and assault. On top of what happened last fall, I'd say the charges are likely to stick."

I nod quickly, but I don't feel any sense of relief. Even with Rich behind bars, Darryn's still going to have to deal with what the bastard's done this time. I hate that it might mean a setback in his recovery—physically *and* mentally.

"Mr. Everson. Grant."

I jerk my head up and my gaze lands on Mr. Kaneko, who's standing to the side of the nurse's desk. I'm on my feet before I realize I'm moving. Coach stands alongside me.

Mr. Kaneko's face is tight, mouth drawn down, and his

shoulders are slumped, but he gives us the tiniest of smiles. "Darryn's doing all right, if you'd like to see him now."

I practically leap to his side as he turns and heads down the hallway. He stops at the third curtained area and holds the hanging fabric back with one hand. "One at a time, and not for long. He's exhausted."

I nod and look at Coach, who motions me forward. I step past Mr. Kaneko and into the small enclosure. The lights are dimmed, but not so much that I can't see Mrs. Kaneko sitting in a chair pulled close to the bed on the other side. She doesn't smile, but she gives me a nod, which I return before I run my gaze over Darryn. The sling on his injured arm is back, and there's a stark red mark on his right cheek that I'd bet was made by a fist.

Rage wells up in my chest—at that moment, I want to rip off Rich's head and piss down his neck. I force the urge away and walk over to the side of the bed. Darryn needs a calm, supportive friend, not a raging maniac.

"Hey, D."

He almost smiles. "Hey, G."

I slide my hand over his forearm, above the new brace on his wrist. "We gotta quit meeting like this."

Darryn laughs and then winces. "Oh man. Don't make me laugh." He nods. "Bruised ribs."

I blow out a breath through my nose, and Darryn must read my anger, because he's quick to reassure me. "I'm fine. Well…I'll be fine." He wiggles the fingers sticking out of the sling. "This thing is a precaution. I have a bruise on my ribs and I'll probably have one on my cheek, but nothing serious."

My eyes fall shut. "I'm sorry. I tried to get to you…"

"It's not your fault." Darryn slides his arm out from under my hand to tangle his fingers with mine instead. My heart beats faster at the affectionate gesture, but I try not to read too much into it. He probably needs the comfort right now.

"They told me you called in the cavalry, man." He lets loose a wicked grin. "If you could've seen the look on Rich's face when the police knocked on his door. I swear he thought he'd just convinced me to go out with him again, that he could take me back to campus and everything would be absolutely fine. He never even thought to check to see if I had my phone on me."

I snort and roll my eyes. "He's not all that bright, is he?"

"Understatement." Darryn's fingers loosen, and his hand falls back to the mattress. "Mmmm. I think the meds are kicking in."

I take a step back, even though all I want to do is stay right there by his side. "I'll let you rest, then. Coach is here. I'll go get him so he can say hi."

Darryn opens his eyes to half-mast. "Thanks, Grant. See ya."

"See ya."

I don't take my eyes off him until I'm out in the hallway and the curtain falls back into place behind Coach. I'm left there with Mr. Kaneko, and I haven't a single clue what to say to him. *Sorry I couldn't keep Darryn from getting hurt a second time?*

To my surprise, he holds out a hand. "Thank you again for looking out for Darryn."

I swallow. "I think this time," I tell him, "Darryn looked out for himself."

Mr. Kaneko pauses and then nods. "He did. I thank you for your help nonetheless." He extends his hand farther, so that I can't *not* take it, not without being rude.

"You're welcome," I force out around the giant lump in my throat. "And thank you."

Chapter Fifteen

Two nights later, I'm sitting on my bed trying to read a chapter for history when the door handle rattles and then turns. I toss aside the textbook and jump to my feet as Darryn walks in, a small smile on his face and his father a step behind him.

"Oh my God, I am so glad to see you." I take a step closer but hesitate until Darryn waves me over.

"C'mon, let's hug it out."

I'm as gentle as I can be, mindful of his multiple healing injuries, but once I get my arms around him, I don't want to let go. Darryn must feel the same way, from the way he relaxes into me and lets out a soft exhale.

God, he smells good.

I want to live in this hug forever, but his dad is *right there.* I force myself to let go and back away. Darryn's arms slide away as slowly as mine, like he's as reluctant to let go as I am.

I nod at Mr. Kaneko, who's watching us. "Sir," I tell him.

He sighs. "I told you, Grant. Call me Ken."

I share a glance with Darryn. "Sorry...Ken." I force the name out. "I spent my entire childhood being taught to call adults Mister and Missus, sir and ma'am. Hard habit to break."

Mr. Kaneko—I'll still going to think of him that way even if I remember to use his first name out loud—sets the duffel bag he's carrying on Darryn's desk. "You're nineteen years old, you and Darryn. You're adults yourselves now."

Darryn winces, but there's laughter in his eyes. "I think I'll stay a kid a little longer. This adulting thing is for the birds."

I grin at him, and he returns it before turning back to his dad. "Thanks for bringing me back, Dad. Tell Mom I promise I'll be super-extra-special careful."

"And I'll keep an eye out for him, too," I put in. "Heck, we'll wrap him in bubble wrap if we have to." I'm only partly joking. If I could put him in a bubble so nothing could hurt him again, I'd do it in a heartbeat.

Mr. Kaneko nods, suddenly serious. "I know you will, Grant. We appreciate everything." He nods again and turns to leave.

Darryn pushes the door mostly shut behind him before he turns around and moves toward his bed. "What'd I miss?"

I feign nonchalance. "Not much, just the usual stuff." I watch as he perches on the edge of his mattress, spine straight, every muscle coiled like he's about to take off down the runway toward the vault. My heart aches to see him so unsure. I sit down across from him and try out a grin. "Tell me, Kaneko. How's it feel to be a self-rescuing superhero?"

Darryn stares at me with wide eyes before he relaxes, and a smile slowly spreads across his face. "I like that," he tells me. "It feels…" He shakes his head. "I don't know. Better. Like maybe now I'm gonna be okay."

My smile softens. "You are." I bite off the entirely inappropriate *babe* my brain wanted to add. *What the fuck, brain? Get a hold of yourself!*

"Anyway." I wave a hand between us. "Let me hear the whole sordid tale. I wanna know all about how you got the drop on Rich the MF-ing Asshole."

Darryn snorts and shifts around until he's got a pillow behind his back and his legs folded up in front of him. I mirror his position.

"He *is* an asshole," he begins. "I know it. You know it." He sighs. "He knows it, too."

I lift my eyebrows, and Darryn goes on.

"He spent high school deep in the closet. And I mean *deep*. Like, he was one of the guys who made fun of the gay kids. He says he never hit them or anything like that." I can't hold back a disbelieving snort, and Darryn tilts his head in acknowledgment. "He said he had too much to drink at a party and started making out with another guy, and he got busted. It was spring of his senior year, so football was over, but all of his friends dumped him."

I bite my lip to keep from saying what I'm thinking. *Sounds like he got what he deserved.*

"Anyway." Darryn shakes his head. "None of that is an excuse, of course. But he told me he was sorry about hurting me and he wanted to say that in person."

I'm gobsmacked by that. "And he thought kidnapping you off the street was the way to go?"

"Yeah, I know." He shakes his head. "I didn't say it made any sense. He seriously didn't seem to think he'd done anything wrong. Not until the police knocked on his door."

Darryn stops there and pulls his knees up close to his chest. He wraps both arms around his knees as best he can with the sling and the wrist brace still in place. It takes all my willpower to stay where I am, when all I want to do is climb into his bed next to him and take him in my arms—not for anything sexual, but for comfort. If I could take away his pain, I would.

"When he realized it was the cops, he freaked out. He started yelling at me and went to grab my arm. I ducked, which is how he hit my face." Absently, he touches his bruised cheek with his fingers. "And then he tried to push me into his bedroom and I hit the doorframe, which is where the bruised ribs came from."

I can't hold in my thoughts any more. "I'd like to slam him into a few doorframes. Fucking asshole."

Darryn meets my gaze, and the fire is back in his eyes. "Oh, don't worry. He got slammed around. I got around him and got the door open for the police. He resisted. Ended up face-first against the wall with his hands twisted up behind his back." Darryn bares his teeth in a parody of a smile. "I'm betting he's been in a world of hurt the past couple of days."

That probably shouldn't make me feel better, but it does. "Good." I sigh. "I just wish he'd gotten his without hurting *you* again."

Darryn makes an abortive move that I think was probably an attempt to shrug before he inclines his head to one side. "I could've done without more bruises, yeah. At least it's not going to set anything back." He waves his splinted arm. "No damage here, and the sling is a precaution. The ribs will be fine in a week or two." He grins. "Not anything worse than I've done to myself in the gym, anyway."

I take a deep breath and then grin back. "How'd you get away to call the cops?"

Darryn smirks. "The biggest cliché ever. Told him I had to pee. Flushed and then turned on the sink when 911 answered."

I laugh outright at that, but there's a knock at our door before I can respond. We both look over to see Pace standing in the partially open doorway, one hand shoved into the front pocket of his jeans and his face creased with concern. "Sorry. I shouldn't interrupt."

He takes a half step back but Darryn stops him. "No, it's fine. Come on in."

Pace pauses and then moves into the room slowly, like he's approaching a time bomb. "I wanted to stop by, see how you were doing." He glances at me. "Both of you."

Darryn gives him the tiniest of smiles. "I'm okay. A little achy and off-balance. I'll be okay soon. Thanks for checking. I appreciate it."

Pace doesn't look convinced, but he nods quickly. "If you need anything…"

Darryn's smile widens minutely. "We'll let you know, promise."

Pace relaxes at that, and he nods again at Darryn, then at me. "You know where to find me."

"Thanks," I tell him. "We'll get that workout thing figured out soon."

"Sure." Pace bobs his head once more. "See you."

He slips back out into the hall, and I stand and follow him to push the door closed. I imagine some others are curious like Pace, but I doubt Darryn wants to spend his evening receiving visitors like a convalescent royal.

"So." I turn back to face him, determined to let everything go for now and treat this like any normal night in the dorm. "Pizza?"

Darryn lets out a sigh that sounded like it came from his toes and falls back against his pillows. "Pizza."

• • •

By the next day, we're about 90 percent back to where we were the week before. Darryn takes a little longer getting ready for class in the morning, but I help him with his backpack as usual, and we make it to our first classes on time. "See you at lunch," I tell him as we split up to head to our different classrooms.

The warmth of his smile carries me through the next few hours, when I drop off my backpack at our usual table in the dining hall and head for the line. I grab two plates and fill Darryn's with some of his favorites—sliced roast beef, mashed potatoes and gravy, green beans, and a yeast roll. I decide to get the same myself and carry both plates back over to the table just as Darryn walks in the door.

"Hey!" I wave him over, and he gives me a puzzled look as he approaches.

"You didn't need to get me a plate," he says as he parks his backpack next to the table.

I shoot him a look. "Not a big deal. You can wait on me next time I get hurt. 'Cause you know that's gonna happen."

He chuckles, conceding the point.

I grin. "I'll grab drinks and stuff. Be right back." I hurry to gather flatware, napkins, and glasses of sweet tea to take back to the table. By the time I get there, Annie's talking to Darryn.

"…was really worried. We're so glad everything turned out okay."

Darryn ducks his head. "Thanks. Yeah. I mean…"

I set everything on the table. "Probably not something he wants to relive."

Annie actually blushes. "You're right. Sorry." She sets her backpack on a chair and then pauses. "Is it okay if I sit with you guys? If you'd rather…"

Darryn looks up at that. "Of course. Please do. But—"

"No talking about the asshole," she finishes, and Darryn tilts his head in agreement.

"Okay then," she says. "Be right back."

I take my seat and catch Darryn's eye to check in with him. "It's okay if you don't want her to sit with us, you know."

Darryn shakes his head. "Thanks, Grant. Really, it's fine.

I like Annie. And from what you said, she helped with the whole…Asshat Who Shall Not Be Named situation."

I snort. "We could call him 'Dick.'"

Darryn almost chokes on his tea. "Oh my God," he says once he clears his throat. "He was adamant that he was *Rich*, too. Not *Richard*, and for God's sake, never, ever *Dick*."

I grin at him. "Dick it is, then!"

Annie's voice cuts in. "Do I even want to know?"

I glance up at Annie, then back at Darryn, and both of us lose it. And does it ever feel good to laugh together again.

Chapter Sixteen

When Saturday rolls around, I do my usual workout with Pace in the morning, then shower and throw on some sweats before settling down to get some classwork done. The space where Darryn usually sits looms empty, though I know he'll be back before long. I'll be glad when he finishes physical therapy so he'll be home on Friday nights.

Home. The thought pulls me up short. But it's how I feel. Even though it's a standard too-small dorm room, sharing it with Darryn is enough to make it feel like a real home.

Sure enough, a little after noon, the doorknob rattles and then the door edges open. "Hey, gimme a hand."

I jump up and step over, reaching for the brown paper bag Darryn's holding out. It's got the logo of a local fast-food place on it, and my mouth waters at the smell of the greasy goodness inside.

"Oh man, I should've done an extra mile on the treadmill this morning," I tell Darryn as he drops his backpack next to his desk. I reach into the bag and pull out a double cheeseburger and a huge container of fries. "Make that five extra miles."

Darryn laughs and slides into his chair. "I talked Dad into running through the drive-through on the way over. I figured you'd appreciate it."

"You have no idea." I've got the burger unwrapped and halfway to my mouth when I realize he's not eating. "Didn't you get yourself something?"

He grins. "Breakfast at the Silver Bullet Diner." He names one of the most popular breakfast restaurants in town. "I'm good."

I chuckle. "For the day, I'd say."

I settle in with my lunch, watching as Darryn digs out a textbook and notebook and spreads his work out across his desk. I know he has a lot of catching up to do, on top of the three regular classes he's taking this semester, so rather than trying to talk, I let him work. I'm finished with my lunch and back into my own notes before he breaks the comfortable silence.

"So," he says, waiting until I turn my head to look at him before he continues. "You free for that dinner tonight?"

I blink once before I remember his comment earlier in the week about taking me out. "You don't have to do that," I tell him one more time, but he shakes his head.

"Yeah, I do. For me as much as anything."

I study his face for a long moment before nodding. "Sure. Whenever you want to go."

"Seven," he shoots back. He follows up with a wink. "And wear something nice. I mean, not fancy nice. Like, khakis and a button-up."

That gets a raised eyebrow from me. I try to play it cool, even though my heart is racing. "Got it."

And then it's back to the books for both of us.

We do take a few breaks from homework during the long afternoon. At one point, Darryn even crawls into his bed and dozes for an hour. Not surprising, considering his body's still healing. I spend my breaks playing phone games and stretching my legs, but by five o'clock, I've burned through pretty much everything I can handle for the day.

I stand up and stretch my arms up over my head, feeling my vertebrae shift and crack from too much time sitting. "Ugh." I let my arms drop. "You'd think they'd spring for some more comfortable desk chairs if they actually expect us to get any work done in here."

Darryn tosses down his highlighter and sighs as he rocks his head from side to side. "I'm just glad they have arms. My shoulder's fine most of the time, but if I leave it unsupported for too long, it really starts to ache."

I wince. "I bet." I step over and sit on the edge of my bed. "How is it most of the time? I mean, really?"

Darryn turns the chair to face me. "I'd tell the doctor the pain's at a two or three on the scale of ten most of the time. More if I've been doing anything more strenuous than sitting or lying down." He shakes his head, a small smile on his face. "I never thought I'd miss being able to wash my hair with both hands."

A quick image of how I could help with that flashes across my mind, but I push it away. "And your wrist?"

He looks down and extends the hand with the brace. "A four to five, usually. I have to use it more, and it was worse to start with, of course. That's down from about a seven. I only need pain meds after PT now." He snorts. "Which is good, because they're trying to get me off them completely. They're stingy about meds now. They don't want me taking anything except Tylenol or whatever."

"Like you being in pain is going to help anything?"

"I know, right?" Darryn shakes his head. "It's enough to have me rethinking my major. I mean, if I'm going to spend all my time working with people who are in pain because the doctors won't give them anything for it…"

Before I can respond, Darryn's phone starts up playing one of its random ringtones, and Darryn reaches over to silence it. "Study session over," he says, tossing me a grin. "Time to get ourselves prettied up and head to dinner."

"Shit." I jump up and head to my closet. "I didn't even think to check to be sure I have something decent that's clean. I think I brought back everything after the holidays."

I go digging toward the far end, where I don't find any khakis, but I do unearth a pair of gray slacks and a light green button-up shirt. I turn to hold them up for Darryn's approval. "I don't need a tie or anything, do I?"

Darryn laughs. "Nothing *that* fancy," he replies. "That'll work great."

"Awesome." I hang the clothes on the hook inside the closet door, dig around on the closet floor for my one decent pair of dress shoes, and then go hunting for clean socks and an undershirt. I don't usually wear undershirts, but in January and with a pretty thin shirt, I'll probably need it.

When I turn back toward my bed with my clothes, Darryn's pulling his out of his closet—navy blue khakis and a blue and white striped shirt. He brings them over to lay them across the foot of his bed and then heads back for the rest.

I watch him for a few moments, an undercurrent of nerves buzzing through me. He sure seems to be taking this seriously, and I find myself wondering… Does he mean this as just a dinner to say thanks? Or is he, maybe, thinking of this as an actual *date*?

No way, I tell myself. *It's gotta be too soon for that. Bring it down a few notches. Darryn is your friend, and he'll stay your friend unless and until he says he wants something more.*

I change into my slacks and undershirt quickly, for some reason feeling awkward about undressing in front of Darryn. I also realize I forgot a belt, so I go looking for that, and by the time I have it through the belt loops and go back for my shirt, Darryn's buttoning up his dress shirt, though he's still wearing his jeans. He's not having an easy time with the buttons, but he's getting the job done. I decide to leave him to it unless he asks for help.

When I finish dressing, Darryn's ready except for his shoes and belt, and he truly is struggling with the belt. I hesitate before I ask, "Need a hand?"

Darryn glances up, his cheeks flushed. "I guess," he says, though he doesn't sound happy about it.

I decide to make it as matter-of-fact as possible. I take the three steps over to stand in front of him, grab the ends of the belt, and slide the buckle together to fasten it as quickly as I can. I ignore how close we're standing—especially the proximity of my hands to a part of his body they would love to touch.

I step away as swiftly as I can. "All good!"

Darryn flashes me that tiny, private smile—there's a light rosy tint to his cheeks that I try not to think too much about—and sits on the bed to slide on his shoes. They're loafers, not lace-ups like mine, so he ends up ready to go before me. I'm only a minute behind him, though.

"There." I stand and hold my arms out to the sides. "Do I pass muster?"

Darryn snickers. "You might want to do something about the hair."

Whoops. I can just imagine what it looks like, considering I barely toweled it dry after my shower this morning and probably ran my hands through it in all directions all afternoon while studying. Sure enough, the small mirror on the closet door tells a tale of infinite woe. Thankfully, a comb, a little control paste, and some well-practiced finger work gets it in manageable condition without too much trouble.

"All right, now I'm ready." I turn back toward Darryn

with a smile, only to find him watching me, eyes soft.

He bites his lower lip and nods. "You look great." He holds my gaze for a few seconds, making my heart and mind race, before he smiles. "Let's go have some good food."

• • •

I pull up in front of the restaurant Darryn directed me to and give him a sidelong look as I put the car in park. "Nice place."

Darryn glances my way. "I've never been. It had great reviews online." He reaches for his seat belt and winces, so I gently nudge his hand away and push the button to release the belt.

"Thanks." Darryn tilts his face up toward mine, bare inches away, and only sheer willpower keeps me from leaning even closer.

"No problem," I say as I move away and reach for my door handle. "Let's see if this place lives up to its online reputation."

Darryn meets me at the front of the car and leads the way inside, although he does let me handle the door without comment. At the host stand, he gives his name, and moments later, we're being escorted to a table for two tucked away in a corner. The restaurant is definitely fancy, despite all Darryn's protests otherwise. Granted, I haven't eaten in anything nicer than a Cheesecake Factory in a couple of years, and that only because Mom loves it, so we usually go for her birthday.

This place is different. It's all low lighting, soft music, candles on each table, with crisp white tablecloths and napkins and servers in near formalwear—black slacks and vests, white dress shirts, and bowties. I'm a little afraid to look at the prices on the menu. I glance around and see most other tables are occupied by couples, or at least, people who appear to be couples.

This isn't the kind of place you take just-a-friend for a simple thank you dinner.

"Relax," Darryn murmurs once we're seated with the menus in front of us. "It's just us."

I must be broadcasting my uncertainty. Sure, it's *just us*, with a setting as thoroughly romantic as this and several hours of high-end dinner service to get through without making myself look like an idiot.

I blow out a long breath and pick up the menu. It's in English, at least, and the prices are high but not ridiculous. That helps me settle a little. It's a start.

Okay, maybe this *is* a date. I can deal with that. Never mind the buzzing that's back in my stomach and the sudden clammy palms at the thought that Darryn is taking me out on a *date*. I'm still playing this the same way. It's Darryn's game, and he decides what happens next.

All I can do is try not to screw things up.

We place our orders quickly, and Darryn fills what might have been an awkward silence—for me, at least—by telling me about the package of Japanese treats his mother's family sent them as a New Year's gift. I'd experienced some of their family's traditions on New Year's Eve, but Darryn tells me that, instead of sending the traditional money, his family filled the envelopes with notes of well-wishes. The rest of the box had been packed with all kinds of Japanese candies and snacks.

By the time Darryn finishes describing the different kinds of treats and promises me a few samples, our meals are nearly finished, though it feels as if no time has passed at all. Our server approaches to refill our water glasses, and as she walks away to get our check at Darryn's request, Darryn lifts his glass.

"I know it's corny," he says, "but I want to make a toast. To you. For being a good friend."

My face heats but I lift my glass anyway. "Same to you."

We clink glasses and sip, gazes meeting in the flickering candlelight. Warmth pools low in my belly, and the longing I'd kept pushed down for months rises back to the surface. *He needs a good friend.* I've been trying to keep my mind focused on that thought, but knowing Darryn's free of that asshole Rich is making it harder every day to keep my feelings to myself. I don't want to rush him into anything. I said I'd wait for him, and that's what I'll do.

The server returns with our check and Darryn makes quick work of payment. I resist the urge to offer to pay my share. He'd made it clear up front that he wanted dinner to be his treat, so I'll let him. I'll make sure I'm the one to take *him* out next time.

Twenty minutes later, we're back in our dorm room, and awkward doesn't begin to cover how I feel. I still don't know if that dinner was a date, but it felt enough like one that I'm not sure how to handle myself now, and Darryn isn't offering any clues. I guess I should get ready for bed like I would any other night?

I step over to my closet and toe out of my shoes, and I'm reaching for the buttons of my shirt—I can wear it at least one more time before it needs washing—when Darryn steps up behind me.

Close behind me.

"Grant, I—" His voice is low, husky. "I want you."

Chapter Seventeen

Darryn's words send a jolt of lust mixed with fear through me. I pivot to face him, but before I can do anything more, he moves in close, wrapping his arms around my waist and pressing his body against mine. My arms come up automatically, and my hands tremble as I skim my fingers across his back.

"Don't ask me if I'm ready," he murmurs against my ear. "I'm not going to pretend I'm not nervous, but I want this. I *need* this. Now. With you."

No pressure, I think, in the instant before he slides his mouth over mine. His kiss is soft but sure, his lips moving with gentle, insistent pressure. I open my mouth on a sigh of *finally*, and he takes the opportunity, bringing his tongue out to stroke lightly against mine. The light touches are intensely erotic, maybe more so than a hard, bruising kiss would have been, and my cock reacts quickly, plumping and filling between us. Darryn makes a low sound deep in his chest and rotates his hips, and I feel his hardness against mine.

Oh my God. I can't believe we're actually here. I can't

believe I get to have this. Have *Darryn*.

Somebody pinch me. I've gotta be dreaming.

I'm trembling all over now, fighting to let him lead this slow, erotic dance. Unfortunately, my actual hands-on experience is limited to a few hurried kisses and one sloppy hand job with a random guy at a high school party. Even so, Darryn's the vulnerable one here. I tamp down my eager body's urge to take charge. This is Darryn's show, and while I'm 1,000 percent in for whatever he wants, it's about what *he* wants. Not about what my libido demands.

Still, I can't help the relief that washes through me when Darryn moans and kisses me harder. He slides his uninjured hand into my hair to hold me close, and I press mine into his back, one high between his shoulders and one low in the curve of his spine. His body molds to mine, and the only thing I want in the world at that moment more is the same position, only with fewer clothes.

He doesn't seem to be in a hurry to move forward. I let myself relax into the embrace and just enjoy kissing him. It's not exactly a hardship, especially not with him wrapped around me like a blanket, warm and solid. After a few more moments, though, my hand slides lower, onto the curve of his ass. It's an unconscious movement, but it yields near-instant gratification when he moans again and presses back into the touch.

He breaks away from our kiss and pins me with his gaze, pupils blown wide with desire.

"I want to touch you," he rasps, and he reaches for my shirt buttons.

Even with the brace still on his wrist, his fingers are nimble, and he has my shirt open and pushed off almost before I can blink. My undershirt is gone almost as quickly, and Darryn spreads his hands out across my chest, ruffling the light dusting of red hair.

He smiles up at me. "I guess the carpet matches the drapes?"

He surprises a laugh out of me, and I slide both hands lower to squeeze his butt. Who cares that he's seen it all in the locker room before? The teasing's too much fun to spoil.

"I guess you'll have to find out, won't you?"

He bites his lower lip and pushes back against my grip again. "I'm looking forward to it."

He lowers his head to lick at my nipple, making my knees go weak. *Damn, fuck, and hell.* At this rate, we're going to be lucky to get me out of my pants before I go off.

As gently as I can manage, I push him away. "Too good," I murmur, bending to press a kiss against his lips. "How about we get naked and get in bed? I don't think my legs are gonna hold me up much longer."

Darryn laughs softly. "I can't promise how long this'll last once we get naked."

I kiss him again. "Me either, but it doesn't matter," I tell him. "Fast, slow, or anywhere in between. As long as it's *us*."

His smile turns soft and he slides his hand around one of mine. "C'mon," he says. "Let's be *us*, only naked and in bed."

"Deal."

He leads me to his bed, which, I realize, has clean sheets and fluffed pillows, not to mention a bottle of lube and a condom on the table nearby. I must have been distracted before we left, if I didn't even notice him getting this ready. The sight of the supplies makes me tremble. Is he ready for that? Hell, I don't know if *I'm* ready for that. Does he even know I'm a virgin?

Doesn't matter. We'll take this one step at a time. No one needs to get fucked tonight.

No promises about tomorrow morning.

Darryn drops my hand and strips off his shirt in a flurry of movement, bringing my attention back to that whole getting naked thing. "Race you," I blurt out, and Darryn laughs again, a sound I'll never get tired of. He's got his shoes kicked off and his pants undone in about two seconds flat, and then I'm hurrying to catch up.

Who wins? Who knows? I could not possibly care less, because Darryn is naked and hard in front of me, and nothing else matters. He takes my hand again and pulls me down onto the bed, lying back to let me roll on top of him. He slips his good hand between us to line up our cocks and then wraps both arms and legs around me.

"God, you feel good." I love the way his voice sounds, raspy and wrecked, but not half as much as I love the way his body feels.

"Can't get close enough," I whisper back. Our mouths are a bare inch apart, our breath mingling. "Never close enough."

He leans up to capture my lips, and I fall in to him again, kissing him hard, tangling my hands in his hair. It takes me some fumbling to find a good angle to brace my knees against the mattress. When I do, I thrust against him, following the move with a deep grind that makes him jerk and moan deep in his chest. I do it again, thrust and grind, and he hikes his legs up higher, crossing his ankles over my ass and pushing me even harder against him.

It's not sex—or, at least, it's not penetration—but it sure as hell feels like it. We find a rhythm by trial and error, friction balanced by the pre-come slicking between us. It's not going to take me long to get there, not when I finally have what I've been wanting for so long. I want to take Darryn over the edge with me, but I can't make myself let go of him long enough to get a hand between us to help.

From the noises he's making, I don't know if that'll be a problem, though. I have to pull away from his mouth to catch my breath. I bury my face into the crook of his neck and kiss and lick the tender skin there. That must work for him, too, because his sounds get louder and he tightens his arms and legs around me.

"God. Grant." He moans. "So fucking good."

"Yeah." I thrust again, grind harder. "Wanna make you come."

"Close," he breathes. "Just a little…"

He fades out into another groan and his body starts to shake. I keep up the sweet pressure, rotating my hips in tiny circles, each movement sending another bolt of pleasure through me. I hope he's feeling even half of what I am, because I'm about to break into a million tiny pieces.

Then a guttural groan escapes his body, sounding as if it comes all the way from his toes. His fingernails and heels dig into my back, and he bites down on the meat of my shoulder. I last about two seconds before I follow him right over the edge.

As I catch my breath, I manage to shift to the side to collapse onto the mattress and not Darryn. The last thing he needs is for me to reinjure anything. There's not much room on the tiny bed, so I end up on my side, back to the cold wall. I hardly feel it, my skin still warm and tingling from my orgasm.

An eon later, Darryn turns his head toward me, and our gazes meet. He studies me, eyes flicking back and forth, and he must like what he finds, because a slow, beautiful smile spreads across his face.

"So," he says, voice shaking like he's holding back a laugh. "Was it good for you?"

I growl and carefully clamber back on top of him, biting back a hiss as my still-sensitive cock brushes his skin. "If you have to ask…"

The laugh breaks free. "Rhetorical question!" he gasps out as I slide my hands down his sides, light enough to tickle. He jerks and wriggles. "No tickling! Ahhh!"

I snicker and roll back to the side, flopping against the wall, now feeling the chill from the wall and the come cooling on my stomach. "No tickling, check. Any other hard limits I should know about?"

Darryn curls onto his side and reaches across the space between us to run his fingers across my chest. His injured wrist lies on the mattress. "Needles," he says, laughter still tinging his words. "I never was into the idea of piercings or anything like that, but after the past few months?" He shudders. "I could do without ever facing down a needle again as long as I live."

I lift my hand to settle on top of his where it rests below my collarbone. "I can understand that," I tell him. "I might be in for a tattoo at some point, though."

"Mmmm." Darryn scratches my skin lightly with his fingernails. "Any images in mind?"

I shrug. "Not yet."

It's a little white lie. I have two in mind—my birthdate and Darryn's. I know better than to put someone else's personal information on my body permanently without a lot of time and thought, though. Maybe if we make it to five years together.

It hits me then. We're *together*. Like, for real.

Butterflies explode in my stomach, and I grip Darryn's hand tighter as I meet his gaze. "You know how I feel about you, right?"

Darryn's face goes solemn and he nods slowly, never looking away. "I know. It's the same way I feel about you."

I lean in, and Darryn does, too, and we meet in the middle in a sweet, gentle kiss.

Damn, I love this man. I can't believe how close I came to missing out on all of this, and I'm going to do everything in my power to make sure he's as happy as I am right now.

Even if it takes every day of the rest of our lives.

Chapter Eighteen

Three weeks later

It's the weekend of the Winter Invitational, the first big gymnastics meet of the season. Usually before a meet I'm buzzing with a mix of nerves and excitement, but today I'm eerily calm. I wake up before my alarm goes off, tiptoeing around the room to keep from waking Darryn, fighting off the urge to wake him with more kisses like the ones we'd shared the night before.

You'll blow them all away tomorrow, he told me, and I'll carry those words with me.

After I shower and dress, I head down to the cafeteria for my usual pre-meet breakfast— fruit and yogurt, toast with peanut butter, and orange juice. I hardly taste it, my mind busy playing and replaying my routines, locking them in so I don't have to think about them. It'll be like instinct.

It's still early when I reach the gym, and I'm dressed out and on the floor for warm-ups a few minutes later. I'm so focused on the competition ahead that I don't even hear

Coach Everson approach. I jump when he puts his hand on my shoulder.

"Remember what we talked about," he says. He'd ended our last pre-meet practice two days earlier with a combination pep talk and last-minute instruction manual for today. "Go hard, but pace yourself. You've got a long day to get through. Don't leave everything on the floor your first time around."

I nod. "Got it."

Coach pats my back. "Have a good day." It's his standard line before any competition, not just a platitude but an instruction and a genuine wish. A "good day" means doing our best, putting forth good effort, and finishing strong.

That's the plan, but I'd sure like to make today about more than that.

I have two goals today—getting through all my routines cleanly, and for floor exercise, finish in the top five. It's early in the season, and I'm only a sophomore, but my personal goal for this season is to get on the winner's podium consistently by the last few matches, at least on floor, since that's my strongest apparatus by far. We'll be doing only four apparatus each today, not all six, which means no vault or high bar for me.

I take a seat with my teammates as the officials and coaches go through all the pre-meet discussions. While I wait, I turn and scan the stands, looking for familiar faces. My parents are probably coming later in the day, so I don't expect to see them. I do catch sight of Annie and Mo about halfway up. Annie gives a little wave, Mo a bigger one, and I wave back.

I've moved on to trying to find Darryn when someone taps me on my arm. I turn to find the man himself smiling and sliding into the seat next to me.

"Hey!" I grin at him. "What are you doing down here?"

He waves his arm down his body, and I realize he's

wearing the team athletic suit, gray with blue trim and the gray-and-blue Tornados logo on the chest. "Coach put me on disabled reserve so I could dress and sit with the team. I decided to surprise you."

My smile feels like it'll split my face wide open. "Well, I'm surprised! Glad to have you here."

I'd love to kiss him right now, but I realize that as much time as we've spent together in our dorm room the past few weeks—a lot of it naked—we haven't talked about when and how to go public with our relationship. I do let myself reach over and squeeze his knee for a second, figuring it's a friendly enough teammates gesture not to raise eyebrows.

Darryn raises an eyebrow at me, as if he's read my mind, and he probably has. He bumps my side with his elbow. "You gonna win one for me?" he murmurs.

A flash of heat washes through me. "I'll win it all for you, baby," I whisper back.

The announcer's voice comes over the loudspeaker, drowning out any possible reply, but Darryn mouths *baby?* back at me, and I shrug. *You heard me*, I mouth back.

And then it's time to get down to business.

· · ·

The meet starts out well for us. Heath sticks his difficult dismount from the pommels, Kenny's flairs on the floor look *so* much better than they did back in the fall, and I get through the iron cross on rings without losing it too soon. By the time I walk out onto the floor for my final event, I'm a little tired but pumped and loose.

From the moment I start my routine, I know it's good. My leaps are strong, my landings solid, my flairs high. I can hear the crowd react with each tumbling pass, but it doesn't intrude on my focus. The minute flies by, and after I nail my last diagonal run across the mat—round-off into a double-twisting forward flip punching into back layout followed by a front tucked flip—I hold my last landing before lifting my arms and nodding toward the judges' table. I walk off to the roar of the hometown crowd, and Coach Sato greets me at the bench with a nod and a slap on the shoulder.

"Great job," he says, and that's the biggest compliment I could get. I grin as my teammates congratulate me with low-fives and more shoulder pats. I know my performance was good, probably the best of my career. I just have to wait to see if the judges agree.

A minute later, the score pops up: 14.130. A whoop that sounds suspiciously like Darryn comes from behind me. That's two-tenths of a point higher than my previous top score, the first time I've crossed the 14-point barrier, probably helped by the added difficulty. Hell, that might even be enough to get me into the event finals at nationals, if I can keep it up for the whole season.

The crowd noise spikes, and I look over toward the display where they've posted the apparatus standings. My mouth drops open. My name stands at the top of the list, 0.20 points ahead of Markman from Carlisle U, who probably everyone thought would win—including me. And then Coach Sato is next to me, and I lean in to hear what he's yelling into my ear over the crowd noise.

"If my math is right," he says, "you're at third in the all-around. Congratulations, Clark."

My teammates are swarming me by then, but I'm still stunned. I knew I'd performed well today. I *hadn't* expected to leapfrog over that many great competitors to win my first apparatus and finish so high overall.

Then Darryn's face is in front of mine, the smile on his face blinding. "You did it!"

And just like that, it sinks in.

"Oh my God!" I grab Darryn in a huge hug, and he laughs against my neck. Within seconds, we're the center of a team hug, guys patting me on the back and congratulating me from all directions.

I did it. Holy crap. And it's our first meet. I have a whole season and two more years ahead of me.

But the best part of all is that I'll have Darryn right by my side all the way.

• • •

The awards ceremony goes by in a blur. It isn't exactly Olympics-caliber, but it'll do nicely. I accept the trophy for my first-place floor exercise finish and clap for the other winners. We finish third as a team, which doesn't come with hardware but gives us a big boost going into the rest of the season.

The second the ceremony ends, my teammates surround me again, but I only have eyes for one of them. I reach out for Darryn's hand and pull him close.

"Here." I hold out the trophy. "This is yours."

His eyes widen. "No way!" he protests. "You earned every bit of that."

"It wouldn't have happened without you." I slide my free hand up his arm to cup his nape. "I love you so much."

And I kiss him.

Right there on the floor, in front of my teammates, the other gymnasts, the fans in the stands, my family and friends, God, and anybody else who wants to have a look. It occurs to me after a second that I should have checked with him first, but when I try to back away, he reels me back in.

When we finally break apart and the noise of the crowd filters back in, Darryn's grinning from ear to ear. "I love you, too," he says. "So fucking much. But you keep that plaque. You earned it. Besides." He winks. "A year from now, I'm gonna win some of those for myself."

I laugh as I wrap my arms tighter around him. "Sounds like a plan." I tilt my head to one side. "Now how about we take this celebration somewhere a little more private?"

Darryn's smile turns sultry, and he leans in to touch his lips to mine. "How fast can you shower?"

"With you waiting?" I give him my best medal-winning grin. "It'll be a new personal record."

Acknowledgments

First up, all the love to my accountability group buddies, Sasha Devlin and Dylan St. Jaymes. It might have taken 15 months to get this story to THE END, but I never would've made it there without y'all. Love you, ladies!

Thanks also to my beta readers, Dylan, Dani, and Sarah; to Thea Nishimori for assistance with Japanese-American cultural references; and of course, my editor, Amy Acosta, who helped me shape this book into everything it should be.

Special recognition goes to Nadia Comaneci, who first made me a gymnastics fan, at the tender age of seven and a half, and who (along with her husband, Bart Conner) was kind enough to sign autographs for me during the 1996 Olympics in Atlanta.

Finally, a note in memory of Kurt Thomas, who died in June 2020, while I was working on edits for this book. The first US male gymnast to win a world championship gold medal, he created the "Thomas flairs" that figure into this story.

About the Author

Shae Connor lives just outside Atlanta, where she's a government worker by day and writes sweet-hot romance by night. She's been making things up for as long as she can remember, but it took her a while to figure out that maybe she should try writing them down.

Shae is part Jersey, part Irish, and all Southern, which explains why she never shuts up. When she's not at her laptop, she enjoys cooking, traveling, watching baseball, reading voraciously, giving and receiving hugs, and wearing tiaras. She also serves as director/editor of the Dragon Con on-site publication, the *Daily Dragon*.

Discover more New Adult titles from Entangled Embrace...

Falling for the Player
a novel by Jessica Lee

Bad boy and former NFL running back Patrick Guinness is tired of meaningless sex. Ever since his scorching hot one-night stand three years ago, no one has interested him. So when Max Segreti wanders into his mechanic shop—and his life again—Patrick can't stop thinking about the totally-out-of-his-league law student and the possibility of getting him out of his system once and for all...

The Reality of Everything
a *Flight & Glory* novel by Rebecca Yarros

Morgan Bartley throws herself into the renovation of her dilapidated beach house, trying to put her life back together after the death of the man she loved. She's intent on strengthening the foundation of her home—and her broken heart—to endure whatever storms lie ahead. But she never bargained for her ridiculously handsome neighbor, whose need to rescue runs as deep as her need to conquer her grief on her own.

FULL COUNT
a *Westland University* novel by Lynn Stevens

If I want to keep playing baseball, I need a tutor. I don't know what—or who—I expected, but it sure as hell wasn't Mallory Fine. Quiet, a little intense, my kind of gorgeous Mallory Fine—who hates baseball and any guy who plays it. I tell myself this is only a tutoring relationship, but I'm a liar. Mallory might be a challenge, but so is getting back on the ball field and I'm determined to make that happen—no matter the cost.

BEYOND THE STARS
a novel by Stacy Wise

College-student Jessica Beckett should be spending her junior year in France, eating pastries and sharpening her foreign language skills, but instead she's stuck babysitting Jack McAlister, Hollywood's hottest heartthrob. He's private, prickly, condescending—and makes it very clear he doesn't want a personal assistant. Sparks fly as they push each other's buttons, and soon Jessica is wondering if a sexy, successful guy like Jack could ever find love with a regular girl like her.

Made in the USA
Coppell, TX
21 October 2022

85065053R00118